REVELATION

Study Bible
(Red Letter Edition)

True Believers' International Version

TBIV

cTom

ISBN:
ISBN-13: 978-1533202161
ISBN-10: 1533202168

Table Of Contents

.

.

.

.

.

.

.

.

FOREWORD

Revelation is the last book in the Bible. The book says it was written by John, while living on Patmos Island. Except for this, we do not know anything about the author. The legend says that he was a disciple of Jesus and he wrote the 'Gospel of John'. Disciple John, son of Zebedee, was an illiterate fisherman from Galilee who spoke Aramaic. Disciple John could not even write Aramaic let alone Greek. Gospel of John is a compilation of sayings of Jesus written by a literate Greek. It was written in third person, several decades after death of Jesus and the spread of Paulian Christianity, between 90 and 110AD. Gospel of John was not written by a disciple of Jesus. The language styles of Gospel of John and book of Revelation are different and their authors are different.

The legend says that John was banished to Patmos Island and there he received a revelation from Angel Gabriel while sitting in a cave. Hundreds of years earlier Daniel claimed that he received a revelation from Angel Gabriel. Daniel was told what will happen in the near future, during a period of 70 weeks. This turned out to be a false prophecy as none of that happened. Book of Daniel is the creation of unknown authors and Prophet Daniel is most probably a fictional character. In 600 AD, Prophet Mohammed received a revelation from Angel Gabriel when he was sitting in a cave called 'Hara Hira' near Mecca, in Arabia. Mohammed's story is well documented and corroborated and historic. So, there is in fact an entity called Angel Gabriel and that it is possible for Angel Gabriel to appear to somebody. However, John has produced nothing to back up his claim of receiving a revelation from a heavenly creature. The book of Revelation is a book of fantasy and it contains no new information and the so-called prophecies that were supposed to happen immediately have not happened in the following 2000 years.

Unlike Daniel and John, Prophet Mohammed continued to receive messages from Angel Gabriel for the next 23 years. Little by little the whole Quran was revealed to him. Quran says that all human beings were created from one pair and all life forms were created from water. Quran accurately described the formation of rain and explained the water cycle. Quran accurately described the stages of human embryonic development. These are only few of the many scientific facts in Quran. All these scientific facts revealed in Quran were discovered by scientists only 1300 years later, in the 20th century, using modern scientific technique and instruments. There are many mathematical formulae in Quran. The word 'day' appears 365 times (even though at the time of Mohammed, lunar calendar was in use and a year had only 360 days). The word 'week' occurs 52 times. The word ‘month’ occurs 12 times. The words 'man' and 'woman' occur equal number of times (men and women are considered equal in Quran). The words 'Adam' and 'Jesus' occur equal number of times (Adam and Jesus were created in similar manner according to Quran). These are just some of the mathematical formulae found in Quran. Because of scientific facts and mathematical formulae in the book, we know that Quran was revealed by a heavenly source. Human beings could not have imagined up such scientific facts 1400 years ago.

The book of Revelation is a jumbled bundle of sayings from (Daniel 9) and (Mathew 24) with psychedelic imagery added to it. No scientific facts are revealed in the book of Revelation. In fact, many unscientific descriptions appear in it. For example the Revelation says, 'one third of the sun was shut off and therefore the sun did not shine on one third of the earth.' The Book of Revelation says: ‘The Serpent (Devil) with its tail pulled down one third of all stars and threw them on to earth’, etc. The book of Revelation predicted imminent destruction of world. After 2000 years, the world is still going strong.

Native American Chiefs used to see visions and they were accurate in many instances. Native American shamans use peyote to enhance their mysticism. Peyote and many other plants contain ‘mescaline’ which create a great psychedelic experience with vivid images and bright colors. Some of the descriptions in the book of Revelation, were most probably generated after Paul ingested 'mescaline' or similar psychedelic hallucinogens found in flora and fauna of Patmos Island.

If God or a heavenly creature had revealed something to John, it would have been some useful information and it would have been given in a straight forward, understandable manner. No such information or revelation is found in the book of Revelation.

Jewish Priests sent Paul to identify and destroy all Jews who followed the teachings of Jesus. Paul could not have identified and killed all Jews who believed in Jesus because many of them were cryptos. Cryptos means they were one thing outwardly (for example Jewish) but another thing secretly (for example Christians). Modern day Turkey have been ruled by Crypto Jews who are outwardly Muslims. Similarly, modern day Saudi Arabia is ruled by Crypto Jews (house of Saud) who are outwardly Muslims. Catholic Church has been usurped by Crypto Jews. The Pope who ordered inquisition and killing of millions of innocent Christians was a crypto Jew. All Popes since 1958 have been Crypto Jews. Muslims are prohibited by their religion to harm Jews or Christians. Jews, on the other hand, teaches to kill Muslims and Christians wherever they can get away with murder. The crypto Jews who rule Turkey massacred 1.5 million Armenian Christians in 1915. Crypto Jews who rule Arabia (house of Saud) have killed millions of Muslims of Arabia. Both Turkey and Saudi Arabia are close allies of Israel.

Paul used a unique technique called 'embrace and corrupt' or 'embrace and enhance' to persecute the Jews who believed in Jesus. The same technique was used successfully by Microsoft Corporation to kill off all its competition. Paul infiltrated the Christian ranks by claiming that Jesus talked to him. After, thus gaining acceptance among Christians, he corrupted all their beliefs and made them all idol-worshippers and blasphemers and therefore ineligible to enter heaven.

Jesus came only to save Jews from their filthy Talmud (which Jesus called 'traditions of Elders') (Mt.15:1-20). Jesus specifically instructed his disciples not to enter the non-Jewish (Samaritan) cities to preach (Mt.10:5). Jesus refused to heal the daughter of a Cananite woman (Mt.15:21-28) and compared her to a dog (a filthy, poop-eating animal). Non-Jews are referred to as Goym (filthy animals) even by Khazaris or the so-called European Jews who claim to be Jews but are not. Contrary to the teachings and orders of Jesus, Paul converted non-Jews into Christianity. He did away with the Jewish customs of circumcision and prohibition against eating pork and observance of Passover and other Jewish holidays. And worst of all, Paul taught Jesus was god and he made all Christians to worship Jesus. Worshipping someone other than the one-and-only-God-in-heaven is idol-worship and contrary to the first commandment. Jesus said that one must obey all the commandments to enter heaven. Thus, by making Christians to worship Jesus as God, Paul made them idol-worshippers and blasphemers. Idol-worshippers and blasphemers shall not enter the kingdom of God promised by Jesus.

Author of the book of Revelation claimed that he saw Jesus and that Jesus commanded him to write the book of Revelation. After, thus taking Christians into confidence, John twisted some of the sayings of Jesus and introduced Greek mythological concepts into Christianity. According to John, Jesus earned immortality by surviving the tribulations in his life. In Revelation, Jesus and God are separate and distinct entities and Holy Ghost is nowhere to be found. In Revelation, Heaven is a copy of the world on earth. Those who are taken to heaven eat, drink, wear clothes and jewelry, hold palm leaves and sing, wear crowns, write names in foreheads, make wars, rides on horses, flies on wings of birds, smoke rises up, light is needed to see, etc. Jesus said, after resurrection people become like angels and not like humans (Mt.22:30). Both John and Paul have been successful in hijacking and corrupting the teachings of Jesus.

For ordinary reader, the book of Revelation reads like a fantasy adventure. He made seven copies of his book and sent to seven nearby churches. Making seven copies was a major effort in those days and was equivalent to printing million copies on a personal printer at home in today's world. Why would he send books to Asian church congregations instead of to larger and powerful congregations in Rome, Syria and Egypt? In those days, those Asian Christian communities lived in isolation and were superstitious and they had no way of validating the book. If the book of Revelation was sent to established churches, it would have been rejected.

The book of Revelation says that God and Jesus sitting on a throne in heaven are concerned only about the seven church congregations in Asia. The Asians believed it and were flattered by their special position. They didn't want to take a chance with the so-called words or Jesus and the promised blessings and curses written in the book. So they believed it. In 325 AD, when the Nicaea conference rolled around, somebody carried this book to Nicaea. The attendees of the conference failed to notice that none of things that were supposed to happen immediately have not happened in 225 years. The participants of the conference were scared by the claim in the book that it was the words of Jesus and anybody who messes with it will be cut off from the book of life. So they incorporated the book into the bible without validating it.

The book of Revelation continues to undermine Christianity to this day. In modern world, the established Christian churches mostly ignore the book of Revelation. The biggest proponents of the book of Revelation nowadays are the Christian Zionists funded by those Zionists who hate Jesus and his teachings. The Book of Revelation talks about Jesus saving 144000 from 12 tribes (Jews being one of the 12 tribes), and making a New Jerusalem and Temple of God in heaven. Zionists use these imageries to claim that 'Jews' are special people and the modern day city of Jerusalem is the new Jerusalem mentioned in Revelations and that a new temple needs to be built on the location of the Muslim Al Aqsa Mosque to make the rapture (saving) of Christians possible. Such ridiculous interpretations and claims are popularized by corrupt bibles written by Zionist agents Darby and Scofield and propagated by Zionist-funded corrupt so-called Christian preachers. Over 75 million gullible, ignorant so-called Christians claim to be Zionists in modern America. They send their hard-earned money to modern day secular republic of

Israel. With that money Israel continues to demolish ancient churches that still stand in Palestine and burn old bibles that still exist in that country and to confiscate the land and property and homes of Christians and to kill and persecute the Palestinian Christians and Muslims.

Some of the sayings in the book of Revelation came true though. Book of Revelation warns about those who say they are Jews but are not. This is referring to the nomads of Khazaria who converted to Talmudic Judaism around 1000AD. They turned out to be the converts into Judaism which Jesus warned about: twice as devilish as the Jews who were the sons of Satan in times of Jesus. They continue to be the promoters of one world government, New World Order, destruction of morality and worship of God and world banking based on usury and other Satanic agendas.

Book of Revelation warned about the numeric system promoted by agents of Satan identified by 6, 6, 6. Those who are identified with the six pointed star, with six sides and six triangles is the root of all evil in modern society.

Book of revelation warned about a satanic worldwide system where those who are not marked by the digits of Satan are not allowed to buy or sell. In modern world, everything has to be bought or sold by credit or debit cards with a chip in it. Soon everybody will have chips implanted in their body. These chips can be tuned or on or off at will by the central computer making the whole world population slaves of the world bankers, the international Jews.

Angel Gabriel dictated Quran to Prophet Mohammed. Quran is the highest quality literature in Arabic language. Descriptions of complex scientific matters are accurately described in simple language. In contrast, John's mescaline fueled psychedelic ramblings reveals no new information. He was an anti-Jesus, Greek Jew, and he excluded Holy Ghost from heaven.

G. Gennady

PREFACE

We do not know if 'John' was the real name or a pen-name of the author of Revelation. He was definitely Greek. He was not a disciple of Jesus. The book of Revelation is a rehashing of the prophecies that were made over a thousand years ago by (Daniel 9, 10) and the sayings of Jesus in (Matthew 24:3-31, Luke 21: 7-36). John added some psychedelic descriptions to make the apocalyptic scenes more colorful and bizarre. It is possible that John has witnessed the horrors of volcanic eruption at nearby island of 'Thera' ('Santorini'). Book of Revelation contains many graphic descriptions of live volcanic eruptions.

Patmos is a small volcanic island in the Aegean Sea, 37 miles from the Turkish coastal city of Miletus. At the time of John, Patmos was a bustling island city on the sea lane from Ephesus to Rome. The temple of Diana on the island was one of the seven wonders of the ancient world. White clouds, thunder and lightning, great hail and rainbows are commonly visible from Patmos. From the peak of 900 ft. tall Mt. Elias, John had a spectacular view of the Aegean Sea islands to the west and the mountains of Asia Minor (Turkey) to the east. When viewed against the setting sun, the sea appears like a "sea of glass, mingled with fire" as described by John. Volcanic eruptions are usually preceded by earthquakes and loud sounds. During such an eruption in nearby 'Thera' island, small islands could be drowned by tsunamis and the mountains of the mainland could be obscured by ash filled air.

Only one spring exists on the island, and John described it as the "pure stream of water of life, clear as crystal, proceeding from the throne of God and of the Lamb" in the New Heaven and New Earth. John wanted to worship God who created heaven and earth and sea and springs of water.

John could have stood on the Psili Ammos beach, the only beach on the island with light, fine, golden sand, and watched the burning lava from a volcano flow to the sea and become like the beast rising up out of the sea, having seven heads and ten horns, and on his horns ten crowns, and on his heads a blasphemous name. John does not say what it was, because he could not think of a name that would be blasphemous.

There were several volcanic eruptions over the millennia in the island of Thera. Roman historians have described the eruption between 1520 and 1460 BC as the largest in historical times. It destroyed the Minoan civilization on Crete. John could have used this historic eruption as the basis for his seventh bowl judgment: 'a great earthquake, such a mighty and great earthquake as had not occurred since men were on the earth'.

Eruptions in 197 BC, 19 AD and 46/47 AD are well documented by Roman historians. John's descriptions of the judgments in Revelation are similar to eyewitness accounts of these eruptions of Thera.

During volcanic eruption, earthquake, bright sparks shooting up and then falling from heaven like shooting stars and movement of land masses are common. Volcanic cloud would darken the sun and make the moon appear blood-red. John calls it the sixth seal.

John describes hail and fire mingled with blood thrown to earth and destroying one third of the trees and burning up all the grass. The flames issuing out of the sea, noxious vapors, explosions of lava crashing into the sea, burning up of surrounding flora and fauna are common in volcanic eruptions.

John described the second trumpet judgment as: 'something like a great mountain burning with fire was thrown into the sea, and a third of the sea became blood; and a third of the living creatures in the sea died, and a third of the ships were destroyed'. It is usual for the sea in the immediate vicinity of the volcano to become brilliant orange color. Sulfur vapors mixed with the sea can turn it white and cause the fish of the sea to die and wash up on the shore. 150 feet high Tsunami tidal waves associated with earth quakes can make the islands disappear and destroy the ships in the harbor.

If John had not witnessed a live volcanic eruption, he used the descriptions of the volcanic eruptions by Pliny the Elder and Tacitus. In catastrophic events like volcanic eruptions and earthquakes and Tsunamis, people either turn to God or cry out cursing God as John describes.

H. Rosenberg.

INTRODUCTION

Daniel's Apocalypse.

To understand the book of Revelation, one has to understand the vision Prophet Daniel supposedly had (Daniel 9, 10) long ago. Angel Gabriel appeared to Daniel and told him what might happen to his people during the following 70 weeks. Since that was about future and told by a heavenly creature, it is called a prophecy. Since the word 'Messiah' (anointed one) appears in this prophecy, it is called a Messianic prophecy. Unfortunately, 70 weeks came and went and nothing happened. So, it was a false prophecy.

Over the years, apologists have tried to massage the 70 weeks and stretch it into hundreds of years to make it fit some of the historical events. Some of them have changed the seventy weeks into 70 x 7 x 52 weeks (490 years). There is no rhyme or reason to multiply 70 by 7 and then by 52. If Daniel meant 490 years he would have said so. When Daniel said 70 weeks, it meant 70 weeks. When Moses said 10 commandments, he meant 10 commandments, not 10 x 7 x 52 commandments. Daniel's prophecy was clearly about 70 weeks and that prophecy failed. Even if the 70 weeks were stretched to fit destruction of Jerusalem in 70 AD by Romans, it failed because prophecy clearly states that the end of the destruction will be with a flood. There was no flood. In fact, no part of Daniels's prophecy came true.

The biggest proponents of Daniel's 70 week prophecy are Zionists who do not believe in God. They want to use Daniel's prophecy to change public opinion among Christians in America in favor of the modern country called Israel occupying Palestinian lands and horribly oppressing Palestinian Muslims and Christians.

John fashioned his book of Revelation after the prophecy of Daniel. He also added the apocalyptic prophecies of Jesus in Mathew 24 and Luke 21. Then he fictionalized the whole thing with his own colorful psychedelic descriptions derived from mescaline induced fantasy and with borrowed descriptions of volcanic eruptions at 'Thera' island.

(Daniel 9: 20-27) 'While I was speaking, and praying, and confessing my sin and the sin of my people, children of Jacob, and presenting my supplication before God, the man Gabriel, told me: 'O Daniel, Seventy weeks are ordained upon your people and upon your holy city, to finish the transgression, and to make an end of sins, and to make reconciliation for sin, and to bring in everlasting righteousness, and to seal up the vision and prophecy, and to anoint the most Holy.

Restore and build Jerusalem for the Messiah the Prince in seven weeks. The street and the wall shall be built again in sixty two weeks.

Then Messiah shall be killed, but not for himself. The people of the Prince that shall come shall destroy the city and the sanctuary; and its end shall be with a flood, and at the end of the war desolations are ordained.

He shall confirm the covenant with many for one week: and in the middle of the week he shall stop the sacrifice and the oblation, and he shall make it desolate because of the overspreading of abominations, and the place shall be consumed. That decision shall be poured upon the desolate.'

(Daniel 10: 4-12) 'In the twenty-fourth day of the first month, as I was by the side of the great Hiddekel River, I saw a man clothed in linen, whose loins were girded with fine gold of Uphaz. His body was like the beryl, and his face as bright as lightning, and his eyes as lamps of fire, and his arms and his feet were of the color of polished brass, and his voice like the voice of a crowd.

When I heard his voice, I fell asleep with my face to the ground. Then a hand set me upon my knees and on the palms of my hands.

He told me: 'O Daniel, a man greatly beloved, understand the words that I speak to you and stand upright because I am sent to you.' Then I stood trembling. Then he told me: 'Now I have come to make you understand what shall happen to your people in the last days, which shall come after many days.'

Jesus's Apocalypse:

(MT.24: 3-42) 'As he sat on the Mount of Olives, the disciples came to him privately, and asked: 'tell us, when shall these things happen? And what shall be the sign of your coming, and of the end of the world?

Jesus answered: "Pay attention so that nobody deceives you. Because, many shall come in my name, saying, 'I am Christ', and shall deceive many. You shall hear of wars and rumors of wars. Don't be worried because all these things must happen. But it is still not the end.

Tribe shall rise against tribe, and kingdom against kingdom: and there shall be famines, and pestilences, and earthquakes, in diverse places. All these are the beginning of sorrows.

Then they shall deliver you up to be tortured, and shall kill you: and you shall be hated by all tribes for sake of my name. Then many shall be offended, and shall betray one another, and shall hate one another. Many false prophets shall rise, and shall deceive many. The love of many shall grow cold, because sin shall be all around. But those who shall endure until the end shall be saved."

"This good news of the kingdom shall be preached in all the world for a witness to all tribes; and then the end shall come."

"Therefore, when you shall see the abomination of desolation stand in the holy place, as Prophet Daniel spoke, (whoever can read, let him understand), then let those who are in Judea flee into the mountains:"

"Those who are on housetop should not come down to take anything out of his house: Those who are in the field should not return back to take his clothes."

"Misery to those with child, and to those who breastfeed in those days! You pray that your flight be not in the winter or on the Sabbath day."

“Then there shall be great troubles, greater than any that ever happened or will ever happen. Unless those days of troubles shall be shortened no flesh shall be saved. But for the sake of the elect, those days shall be shortened.”

“Then, if anybody tells you, that Messiah is here or there, don’t believe it. Because false prophets and false Messiahs may come and show miracles and wonders, so much so that if it was possible, they shall deceive the very elect. Listen, I warned you. If they tell you he is in the desert, do not go there. If they say he is in the secret chamber of the temple, do not believe it. Because the son of man shall come like the lightning that shines from East to West. Because the eagles shall gather where the dead body is.”

“Immediately after the troubles of those days, the sun shall be darkened, and the moon shall not give her light, and the stars shall fall from heaven, and the powers of the heavens shall be shaken. Then the miracle of the Son of man in heaven shall appear. Then all the tribes of the earth shall mourn, and they shall see the Son of man coming in the clouds of heaven with power and great brightness.”

“He shall send his angels with a great sound of a trumpet, and they shall gather together his elect from the four winds, from one end of sky to the other.”

“Now, hear the parable of the fig tree. When its branch is tender and leaves sprout, you know summer is near. Similarly, when you see these things, know that it is near, and even at the doors.”

“Truly I tell you, this generation shall not pass, till all these things are fulfilled.”
“Heaven and earth shall pass away, but my words shall not pass away.”

“No man, not even the angels of heaven, but my Father only knows of that day and hour. Son of man shall come, like the days of Noah. In the days before the flood they were eating and drinking, marrying and giving in marriage, until the day that Noah entered into the ark, and the flood came and took them all away. The coming of the Son of man also shall be like that."

"Then two shall be in the field; the one shall be taken, and the other left. Two women shall be grinding at the mill; the one shall be taken, and the other left. Therefore, watch, because you do not know what hour your master comes." '

(Luke 21: 7-36) 'They asked him: 'Master, when shall these things happen? What warning will be there before these things happen?' He replied: *"Pay attention, so that you won't be deceived because many shall come in my name claiming: 'I am Messiah'. That time is near. You should not follow them. But when you shall hear of wars and commotions, don't be terrified because these things must first happen, but the end is not yet at hand."*

"Nation shall rise against nation and kingdom against kingdom. Strong earthquakes shall happen in various places and famines and pestilences and fearful sights and great wonders from heaven shall happen."

"But before all these, they shall lay their hands on you and persecute you, delivering you up to the synagogues and into prisons, being brought before kings and rulers for my name's sake. And it shall become a testimony for you. Therefore, decide in your hearts not to think what you shall answer. Because, I will give you words and wisdom which your adversaries shall not be able to contradict or resist."

"You shall be betrayed both by parents and brethren and kinsfolks and friends. They shall kill some of you. You shall be hated by all men for my name's sake. But not a hair on your head shall perish. In your patience you shall possess your souls."

"When you shall see Jerusalem surrounded by armies, then know that its desolation is near. Then let those who are in Judea flee to the mountains; and let those who are in the middle of Jerusalem get out; and do not let those who are in the countries enter into the city. Because, these are the days of vengeance, so that all things which are written may be fulfilled."

"But misery to those who are with child and to those who breast feed in those days! Because, there shall be great distress in the land and wrath on this people. They shall be killed and captured and taken to all nations and Jerusalem shall be trampled over by the Gentiles until the times of the Gentiles is fulfilled."

"There shall be wonders in the sun and moon and stars and distress and perplexity of nations on earth. The sea and the waves shall roar, men's hearts stopping from fear and seeing those things that are happening on earth and the powers of heaven shall be shaken. Then, they shall see the Son of man coming in a cloud with power and great brightness. When these things begin to happen, look up and lift up your heads, because your redemption is getting closer."

He told them a parable: *"Look at the fig tree and all the trees; when they sprout you know that summer is at hand. Similarly, when you see these things happen, you know the kingdom of heaven is close at hand. Truly I tell you, this generation shall not pass away, till all is fulfilled."*

"Heaven and earth shall pass away: but my words shall not pass away."

"Pay attention to yourselves, lest at any time your hearts is overcharged with excesses and drunkenness and cares of this life, and that day come upon you when you are not aware. It shall come as a snare on all that dwell on the face of the whole earth. Therefore, you watch and pray always so that you may be counted worthy to escape all these things that shall happen and to stand before the Son of man."

.

.

.

.

THE REVELATION OF ST. JOHN THE DIVINE

1 STRANGE CREATURE 'ALPHA AND OMEGA' COMMANDS JOHN TO WRITE WHAT HE SEES (RV.1)

RV.1: 1-2 God revealed to Jesus Christ, things that must happen shortly, so that he may show it to his servants. Jesus sent an angel to his servant John. John recorded the word of God and the testimony of Jesus Christ and all things he saw.

[Jesus died and went to heaven. The Father, the one and only God, told Jesus to sit on his right side while he makes his enemies his foot stool. In 70 AD, many of his enemies (Jews of Jerusalem) were slaughtered by Romans, and God made them into a foot stool for Jesus. But a large number of them followed the advice of Jesus and they ran to the mountains and ran away from the fields and never returned to the city, etc. and escaped the slaughter. They eventually regrouped and killed few million unarmed Roman villagers and farmers in the outlying undefended Roman territories in Libya, Egypt, Cyprus, etc. Then, Roman general Lusius Quietus (Kito) defeated the wicked Jews in 120 AD. The revelation was written between 90 and 100 AD.

God the father told Jesus, what is going to happen in the future. When Jesus was still on earth, his disciples asked him when would the world end. Jesus did not give a specific date but gave some signs of end-times. Jesus sent a vision to John through an angel. Because of this, many people assume that John was a disciple of Jesus. Visions are not always straightforward. John wrote down what he understood from the vision.]

RV.1: 3 He who reads this prophecy and those who hear it and follow what is written in it are blessed because the time has arrived.

[A special reward is attached to this prophecy. All those who read it or hear it being read and follow what is written in it will receive an unspecified reward. Because the time has arrived, the show is about to begin.]

RV.1: 4-6 From John to the seven churches in Asia: 'Grace and peace, from eternal God and from the seven Spirits which are before his throne and from Jesus Christ, be upon you. Jesus is the faithful witness and the first begotten of the dead, and the prince of the kings of the earth and he loved us and washed us from our sins with his own blood and has made us kings and priests to God. Let fame and authority be his for ever and ever. We agree.'

[This is a letter from John to the seven Church congregations in Asia Minor (Modern day Turkey). The author identifies himself as John, one of the million Johns around there. People generally believe, John wrote the 'Gospel of John' also. But, the author of the Gospel of John is anonymous. Gospeler John said he used material written by a favorite disciple of Jesus, to give authenticity to his work. But he did not identify who was that favorite disciple. Judas was a favorite disciple. Jesus took bread and dipped in sauce and put it in the mouth of Judas, during last supper, to show his special affection for him. But Judas did not write anything. Simon called peter was also a favorite disciple. But he was illiterate. The modern scholars (who are mostly non-believers and Zionists) believe the epistle attributed to Peter was not written by him. Author of Revelations identifies himself as John. If he had written Gospel, he would have identified himself there also.

Grace and peace from God and from the seven spirits that stand in front of God and from Jesus is being sent as a special gift along with the letter.

Jesus is a faithful witness, which means he remember everything he see and hear and can recount everything perfectly and therefore he is a faithful witness. Human witnesses usually embellish things or forget details. Jesus sent this message to John. Since Jesus is a faithful witness, everything in this message is exactly as what was revealed to Jesus by God.

Jesus is the first begotten of the dead. God had begotten many sons, as described in the bible. But Jesus was the first that was begotten (sexually reproduced) from the dead (dead people)? This is one of many scribal errors (nonsensical sentences) in handwritten book.

John says that Jesus is the prince of the kings of the earth. It means that he is either king over all kings or heir to the throne of all the kings of earth. So, his kingdom is in earth. That is John's personal opinion. Jesus told Pontius Pilate that his kingdom is not of this world.

Jesus loved us and he washed us with his blood and cleaned us and made us kings and Priests to god. Jesus neither did nor said any such thing. This is purely an invention of John.

Washing in blood is synonymous with anointing. Kings and Priests were anointed. According to John, Jesus did away with the priestly caste (Levites) and made each and every one of the Christians 'kings and priests to God'. No more need to give any money or tithe to the old fashioned Jewish priests. But that is John's personal opinion. Jesus said that he did not come to change the Jewish Law and even a tittle of that Law shall be obeyed until end of the world. Jesus told the Lepers to show themselves to Priests and pay for sacrifices as required by Moses's Law.

John says Jesus washed everybody with his blood and thereby anointed everybody and made kings and priests of god. If true, this will create a lot of kings with no subjects. All chiefs and no Indians. Or, an Al Qaeda situation: US Presidents said every dead person in Afghanistan and Iraq was second-in-command of Al Qaeda to justify their war of aggression against Afghanistan and Iraq. There are no soldiers in Al-Qaida; only second-in-commands. That made sense to the American Public which is known to be dumbed down by drinking poisonous fluoride in their water since birth and being kept mentally retarded by injections of tainted vaccines and kept stupid by common core education system.

Making everybody priests to God is understandable. They can perform sacrifices to God. But what was the significance of making kings to God? Are kings special in the eye of God? Is there special status for kings in the mind of God? If kings are ordinary men with a title, and if titles make no difference in the eyes of God, why would John say God made everybody kings? It is obvious that John just threw in a few heavy words to make the Christian peasants feel good about themselves. After listening to John's letter, they will all be going back to their humble huts thinking that they are kings.

Last part of the verse says: 'Because Jesus has made us priests and kings, we say, let the fame and authority belong to Jesus for ever. Everybody agree.' Again, this is John's personal opinion.]

RV.1: 7 Look, he comes with clouds; and everybody including those who pierced him, shall see him, and relatives shall wail because of him. We agree.

[This is not part of revelation (what Jesus revealed to John). This is John's personal opinion.
John says that Jesus is coming in the life time of those who pierced him: the soldiers who put nails on his hands and legs and the soldiers who pierced his chest. Or, those who pierced him shall not die until the second coming. If the latter is true, then we might have some two thousand year old men walking around among us. But why are these soldiers being punished? They were only obeying their orders. According to John, the Jews got away with murder of Jesus and the soldiers would be punished.

Nobody knows why all relatives and kindred are wailing when Jesus comes with clouds. May be they are afraid of retribution by Jesus. One of the Samaritan cities, refused entry to Jesus and companions, and angry disciples asked Jesus if they should curse the Samaritan city and ask god to send fire and brimstone upon them as punishment. Jesus answered that he came to save lives and not to destroy them. If that is true, there is no need to be afraid of retribution by Jesus. He will be trying to save people, not to punish them.]

RV.1: 8 God said: "I am Alpha and Omega, the beginning and the ending, which is, which was, and which is to come - the Almighty".

[John was not present when God said this. If God had to tell this to Jesus that means Jesus did not know until this time that it was God who was sitting next to him. Then Jesus told his messenger Angel that God said this. Then the Messenger Angel told this to John. Then John wrote it down. It is highly unlikely that Jesus did not know it is God on whose right hand side he is sitting. It would be silly for God to say that to Jesus, his son, after he has returned to heaven to make his enemies his foot stool. So, it is only logical to assume that John made up this statement for the benefit of those who read or listen to his letter.

Did God say that he is alpha and omega? Alpha and Omega are first and last letters of Greek alphabet. If God is Alpha and Omega then he has a beginning and an ending. Anything that has a beginning and an ending cannot be God. It is strange that God would tell Jesus who spoke Aramaic and Hebrew, that he is two characters in Greek alphabet, an alphabet which Jesus was not familiar with. Then the angel transmitted that statement to John. If John was son of Zebedee, disciple of Jesus, he would not have understood this, as he was an Aramaic-speaker. God should have spoken: "I am the God of Abraham, Isaac, Jacob, Moses and Jesus." Instead God spoke: "I am Alpha and Omega". That means John of Patmos was Greek.]

RV.1: 9 I am John. I am your brother and companion in tribulation and in the kingdom and patience of Jesus Christ. I was in the Patmos Island. I was waiting for the word of God and for the testimony of Jesus Christ.

[So, John was waiting for a word of God and for a testimony from Jesus, in the Patmos Island. John makes it sound like God and Jesus are his pals.]

RV.1: 10-11 I was in the Spirit, on the Lord's Day, and I heard behind me a loud voice, like a trumpet, saying: **"I am Alpha and Omega, the first and the last. You write in a book what you see and send it to the seven churches which are in Asia: to Ephesus, Smyrna, Pergamos, Thyatira, Sardis, Philadelphia and Laodicea."**

[John was in the spirit of God, on God's day, which is Saturday, the seventh day, and the day of rest. In 325 AD, Emperor Constantine adopted Christianity and Romanized it and made Sunday, the Roman Day for worship of Sun God, the official Christian Lord's Day.]

RV.1: 12-16 I turned to where the voice came from and I saw seven golden candlesticks. In the middle of the seven candlesticks, someone who resembled the Son of man stood wearing a garment that went down to the feet and girt near the breast with a golden girdle. His head and his hairs were white like wool, as white as snow; and his eyes were like flame of fire; and his feet like fine brass, as if they burned in a furnace; and his voice as the sound of many seas. He had in his right hand seven stars and out of his mouth went a sharp two-edged sword and his appearance was like bright sun.

[John plagiarized the description in (Daniel 10:6) to describe the son of man here. When Jesus lived on earth as Son of Man, he did not look like this fierce creature.

John saw seven candle sticks. In the middle of the seven candlesticks (we are not told if the candle sticks were lighted) stood somebody who looked like 'Son-of-Man'. John is claiming that he knows what son of man looks like. (This is the basis for Christian apologists to claim that John was a disciple of Jesus.) His head and hair was white as snow and flames were coming out of his eyes. He was wearing a garment girted around his breasts and it went all the way down to his feet and his feet were burning brass. If he was bright like sun, can anyone notice all these details? John identified this figure as similar to 'son of man'! This does not resemble Jesus.

He has the voice of a many seas. John heard a loud voice, like a trumpet.

Then he looked back and saw a creature that was bright like sun, but all fine details were visible. If you look at sun, can you see any details? The creature has not spoken yet. Based on his appearance alone, John guessed his voice was like the sound of crashing waves from many seas!

Previously he heard a sound like that of a trumpet. He shone like bright mid-day sun. A two-edged sword stuck out of his mouth. He had seven stars in his right hand. So, this strange figure is 'Alpha and Omega'. Hmmm! Many Christian apologists claim this is figurative. But John meant it literally. The voice commanded John to write in a book what he saw. The voice did not command him to describe what he saw in figurative speech.]

RV.1: 17-20 When I saw him, I fell unconscious at his feet. He laid his right hand on me saying: "Do not fear. I am the first and the last: I am he who lives and was dead; and, look, I am alive for evermore, Amen; and I have the keys of hell and of death. Write the things which you have seen and the things which are seeing and the things which you shall see. The seven stars you saw in my right hand are the angels of the seven churches. The seven golden candle sticks which you saw are the seven churches."

[When John saw this creature, he fell unconscious at his feet. So, this creature was standing very close to him. Even though he was unconscious, he saw the creature reaching out and touching him with his left hand (he was holding seven stars in his right hand) and John, though unconscious heard the creature say that he was first and the last etc.

Did Jesus say: 'I am alive for evermore, Amen'? That is strange. Amen means we agree. When somebody make a statement, the whole congregation may say 'Amen' (we agree). But why would Jesus say that? Jesus never said 'Amen' when he was on earth. Strange!

This 'Alpha and Omega' figure was dead and is alive now and will live for ever and he possesses the keys to death and hell. This is definitely not God. Because God cannot die. Death has a key? This must be Jesus. Jesus died and came back to life and will live for ever. Lazarus and many others died and came back to life and then they died again.]

2 JESUS DICTATE LETTERS TO CHURCHES OF EPHESUS, SMYRNA, PERGAMOS AND THYATIRA(RV.2)

RV.2: 1-7 “Write to the angel of the church of Ephesus: ‘the one who holds seven stars in his hands and walks in the middle of seven golden candle sticks says: ‘I know your works and your labor and your patience and how you can’t bear those who are evil. I know that you have tried those who say they are apostles but are not, and have found them liars. I know that you have suffered and have patience and for my name’s sake have labored and have not fainted. Nevertheless I hold something against you: that you have left your first love. So, remember from where you have fallen and repent and do the first works; or else I will come to you quickly and will remove your candlestick out of its place.’
You and I both hate what the Nicolaitans do.
Let he who has ear, hear what the Spirit says to the churches: ‘I shall give to him who overcomes, to eat of the tree of life, which is in the middle of God’s paradise.’ ”

[This creature did not say it was God. People generally believe it was Jesus. But Jesus was not a creature with a sword sticking out of his mouth and fiery eyes.
It said, ‘God’s paradise’. That means God is a separate person and this creature is not God.

It commanded John to write what it dictates. This is similar to the Angel Gabriel asking Prophet Mohammed to recite what he was told. Prophet Mohammed was illiterate so he could not have written anything down. So, he had to remember what was told and then repeat it later so that other people could write it down. Prophet Mohammed saw Angel Gabriel in many different forms. He was seen sitting on a chair and he filled the whole horizon. He was seen with many wings. He was seen riding a white horse, etc. So, it is possible that such an angel or another heavenly creature has appeared to John in this horrible form.

In Hindu mythology, both Gods and devils can assume various forms.

Gods rarely assume grotesque forms, whereas devils may take grotesque forms like the one described by John. So, it is possible that John saw a Hindu devil in a grotesque form. That can explain why it did not identify itself in plain words, but using a riddle. Hindu Devils are known to play that kind of word games. Otherts may believe that he was one thing by one interpretation, while he is another according to another interpretation of the riddle. Instead of saying, 'I am Jesus', this creature said: 'I am alpha and omega, was dead now alive etc.' .

This church, meaning this group of believers, did a lot of good deeds, but they have forgotten their first love: spreading the gospel. They have listened to many who claimed to be apostles of Jesus but were not. That means in those days there were many false apostles. It is possible that John himself was such a false apostle. When thief comes in Police uniform, what can poor victims do?

In modern days, there are a lot of preachers who preach the devils' interpretation of Bible, like the Mormons and seventh day Adventist, and Jehovah's witnesses and Christian Zionists and thousands of preachers spreading the false gospel of NIV.

Many Christians believe he was one of the twelve apostles of Jesus even though the chances of any of the twelve living past 90 AD and speaking Greek and reading and writing in Greek is remote.

This creature is offering the fruit of the 'Tree of life' from God's paradise to eat and become immortal, to anyone who overcomes the trials and tribulations of the church. God's paradise is still in existence. It had the tree of life in the middle. God created Adam to prune and take care of the garden of paradise. God expelled Adam and Eve from that garden to prevent them from eating its fruits and become immortal.

After Adam was expelled who took care of it all these years? That garden must be all over-grown and become like a forest by now. But the tree of life is still flourishing there.

Are there gardens and trees in Paradise or heavens? Angel Gabriel took

Prophet Mohammed from Mecca to Jerusalem on a heavenly mule-like-creature called 'Al Buraq'. From the 'Masjid on the rock' in Jerusalem, Gabriel ascended with Mohammed to the seven heavens. There, Prophet Mohammed saw a giant tree called 'Sidrat al-Muntaha', a very big lote-tree, on the boundary of the heavens. It had giant fruits and leaves. The colors of the tree were different from anything Prophet Mohammed had seen in this world. If Prophet Mohammed had seen with his own eyes rivers and trees in heavens, the 'tree of life' which the creature described to John must also be true.]

RV.2: 8-11 "Write to the angel of the church in Smyrna: 'The first and the last which was dead and is alive says: 'I know your works, and tribulation, and poverty, (but you are rich) and I know the blasphemy of those who say they are Jews, and are not, but are the synagogue of Satan.'

Fear none of those things which you shall suffer: look, the devil shall cast some of you into prison, so that you may be tried; and you shall have tribulation ten days. You be faithful to death and I will give you a crown of life.

Let he who has an ear hear what the Spirit says to the churches: 'He who overcomes shall not die a second death.' "

[Here, the creature identifies itself as a spirit. So, this is definitely not Jesus and not God. This is a spirit, which means a spiritual creature. Prophet Mohammed said that God created man and angels and devil and many other creatures which we are not aware of. So, this must be one of those spiritual creatures.

Members of this church, who overcome the trials and tribulations and remain faithful to Jesus until death, are offered a crown of life and protection from second death. Life in hell is generally interpreted as second death. Bible says that it is appointed that every man shall die once. If Adam had eaten the fruit of the 'tree of life' when he had a chance while he was still in paradise, men would not have to die. The whole human race must be cursing Adam for what he didn't do.

On the other hand, if Adam had eaten the fruit of the tree of life and become immortal the writer of these stories would have figured out another way to make him mortal to explain the decay and death everybody see every day all around.]

RV.2: 12-17 “Write to the angel of the church in Pergamos: ‘the one with sharp double edged sword says: I know your works and where you live, even where Satan’s seat is: and you holds fast my name, and have not denied my faith, even in those days in which Antipas was my faithful martyr, who was slain among you, where Satan lives.

But I have a few things against you: because you have there those who hold the doctrine of Balaam, who taught Balac to cast a stumblingblock before the children of Israel, to eat things sacrificed to idols, and to commit fornication. You also have those who hold the doctrine of the Nicolaitans, which I hate.

Repent; or else I will come to you quickly, and will fight against them with the sword of my mouth.

Let he who has an ear hear what the spirit says to the churches: I give to him who overcomes, the ‘hidden manna’ to eat, and will give him a white stone with a new name written which no man knows except the one who receives it.”

[Balaam, a God mentioned in the Old Testament, was brought out into this church. Jews were the enemies of Christianity from the very beginning. Apparently some wicked anti-Christian Jews made the Christians eat food offered to Balaam and commit immoral sexual acts. Not all the church members were misled. Some members held on to their faith and overcame that temptation.

The church had some good things going for it, like hating the Nicolaitans. Who were they and what did they do? Nobody knows. But from the context, many Christian apologists have suggested that they tempted Christians to eat food sacrificed to Balaam and commit immoral sexual acts.

That is how the secret societies like the Free Masons and Skull and bones initiate the new members. They are made to commit horrible crimes like child rape (pedophilia), homosexuality, bestiality and murder of children as sacrifice to Satan etc. These acts are photographed and otherwise recorded and kept secret. If the member ever leaves the group, this evidence will be brought out against them and their careers and lives will be ruined. When Donald Trump was running in primary election for the candidacy of Republican Party, in 2016, the veteran politician Newt Gingrich said that the republicans hate Trump because he is uncontrollable and they do not know how to deal with him because he has not been through the initiation process and he never joined the secret societies. Nobody can become anybody in US politics without joining secret societies (Free Masonry, Skull and Bones, etc.). Because the Free Masons who control the whole political process will not allow any uninitiated person to win an election or occupy an important position. That is how they control all the politicians and through them the whole country and through it the whole world.

Once these immoral or sinful acts are committed the Christians will be distanced from their church communities and lost for ever. God has been keeping an eye on those Satanists who were misleading Christian believers. Jesus promised that he will not allow the sheep given to him to be plucked from his hand and God will not allow that to happen (John 10: 25-30). Then how come these Christians were misled by Satanists? Jesus was only talking about his disciples and not about the believers in general. Moreover, Jesus did not keep that promise about his own disciples either. For example, Judas Iscariot was misled by Devil. So, one has to wonder if Jesus really made those promises.]

RV.2: 18 "Write to the angel of the church in Thyatira: 'the Son of God, with eyes like flame of fire, and feet like fine brass, says:

[The creature identifies itself as the son of God. God has sons by the tons. 'Son of God' means a pious person. This creature is deliberately trying to mislead the readers because it does not say which of the sons of God. In the beginning John wrote that God, who is in heaven, told Jesus who is sitting on the right hand side of God, the things that are about to happen. Jesus sent an angel to convey the new information to John who was in Patmose island. The word Angel means 'messenger' in Greek. The scriptures were written in Greek. This particular messenger has been evasive in his identification so far.]

RV.2: 19-29 "I know your works and charity and service and faith and your patience and your works; <u>and the last to be more than the first.</u>

In spite of that I have a few things against you: because you allow that woman Jezebel, who calls herself a prophetess, to teach and to seduce my servants to commit fornication and to eat things sacrificed to idols. I gave her opportunity to repent of her fornication and she did not repent.

Look, I will throw her into a bed and those who commit adultery with her into great misery unless they repent of their deeds. I will kill her children with death and all the churches shall know that I search the thoughts and I will give to every one of you according to your works.

But to you and to the rest in Thyatira I say: 'as many of you do not have this teaching and have not known the Satanic teachings, I will put on you only this burden: You hold on to what you already have till I come.

To him who <u>overcomes and keeps my works to the end, I will give power over the nations: he shall rule them with a rod of iron</u> as I received from my Father and he shall break them to pieces like vessels of a potter. <u>I will give him the morning star.</u>

Let he who has ear hear what the Spirit says to the churches."

[What will anybody do with the morning star, Sirius, which is 8.5 light years away?
The question is would a God who created this whole immense universe care about a poor woman trying to make ends meet with fornication? And try to kill her children with sudden unexplained deaths for her sins? Apparently he would.

When Ayisha, Prophet Mohammed's wife, was accused of impropriety, God intervened and revealed verses of Quran to exonerate her. Ayisha said that she did not know that she was important enough to be mentioned in Quran by God almighty for people to recite until end of times. So, God does care about what every human being does. Anti-Muslim skeptics may say that Prophet Mohammed just made up those verses to protect his wife. But, it can't be so. It had to be revealed by God himself. Because if those verses are removed from Quran, the numerical miracles of Quran will not exist. The numerical miracles in Quran prove that it came from heaven. Because no man could have written such a book over 23 year period keeping track of those mathematical formulas.

This creature (presumed Jesus) promises to make a man from the church congregation of Tyatira, who has overcome his trials and tribulations until the end, a king. He is going to rule the tribes with a rod of iron. If he overcame until the end, that means, he died. So, he is going to rule tribes in heaven?]

.
.
.
.
.
.
.
.
.
.
.
.
.
.
.
.
.
.
.
.
.
.
.

‘

Slander of Ayisha.

Ayisha accompanied Prophet Muhammad on a campaign. She accidentally got separated from the caravan and was stranded in the desert. Safwan, who was travelling separately from the army, saw her sitting alone under a tree. He brought his camel and made it kneel and she got on the camel. Then he walked leading the camel until they caught up with the army.
When people saw Safwan and Ayisha together, people suspected misconduct on their part. Abdullah bin Ubayy fabricated a rumor about Ayisha and spread it. He was the leader of the hypocrites. Some Muslims believed the rumors.
Ayisha fell ill from the journey and was bedridden and she did not know anything about the rumors. She noticed that the Prophet was aloof from her. She heard about the rumor from another woman. Ayisha asked Prophet’s permission and went to her parents’ home. She said: "Rumors about this slander went on spreading in the city for about a month, which caused great distress and anguish to the Holy Prophet. I cried due to helplessness and my parents were sick with mental agony.”

For one whole month, Prophet Mohammed was worried. Then he visited her at her parents’ house. He sat near her and said: “Ayisha, I have heard this about you. If you are innocent, I expect that God will declare your innocence. But if you have committed the sin, you should offer repentance, and ask for God’s forgiveness; when a servant of God confesses his guilt and repents, God forgives him."
Ayisha’s tears dried up. She looked up to her father Abu Bakr who sat nearby. He said, `Daughter, I do not know what I should say’. Her mother Umm Ruman who sat next to him also did not know what to say. Then Ayisha said: ‘You have all heard something about me and believed it. Now if I say that I am innocent – and God is my witness that I am innocent – you will not believe me; and if I confess something which I never did – and God knows that I never did it – you will believe me. I cannot but repeat the words which the father of Prophet Joseph *(Jacob)* had spoken: ‘fa-sabrun jamil’ *(I will bear this patiently with good grace)*.”

Then prophet Mohammed received a revelation, vindicating her and proving her innocence. People around could tell, when prophet Mohammed was receiving a revelation: he would perspire profusely, even in cold weather. Then, he said: "Congratulations, Ayisha, God has sent down proof of your innocence". He recited the following ten verses of Sura An-Noor (24:11-21) that had her vindication:
'Those who brought forward the lie are a group among yourselves: think it not to be an evil to you; On the contrary it is good for you: every one of them will be punished for the sin that he earned, and the punishment will be severe for their leader.'
When they heard it, why did not the believers say 'This is an obvious lie'? Why did they not bring four witnesses to prove it? When they have not brought the witnesses, they became liars in the sight of God.
Were it not for the grace and mercy of God on you, in this world and the Hereafter, a grievous punishment would have seized you, if you had rushed into this affair.
You said things of which you had no knowledge; and you thought it to be a light matter, while it was most serious in the sight of God.
When you heard it, why didn't you say: 'It is not right of us to speak of this: Glory to God! this is a most serious slander'?
God admonishes you, so that you may never repeat such conduct, if you are true Believers.
Those who love to spread scandal among the Believers will have a grievous Penalty in this life and in the Hereafter.
Were it not for the grace and mercy of God on you, you would have been ruined. God is full of kindness and mercy.
O believers, do not Follow the footsteps of Satan. Satan will make his followers commit immoral sexual acts and disbelief and polytheism. And had it not been for the Grace of God and His Mercy on you, not one of you would ever have been pure from sins. But God purifies whom He wills, and God is All-Hearer, All-Knower."

The slander of Ayisha, the mother of all believers, was a serious crisis among the Muslim community. Three Muslims who were proven guilty got punished. Guilty among the hypocrites were spared.

When people told about 'Hassan bin Thabit' who spread slander, Ayisha acknowledged his service to Islam more than his role in her slander and said: `...he was the one who used to rebut the anti-Islamic poets on behalf of the Holy Prophet and Islam'.

Abu Bakr used to financially support his relative, Mistah bin Uthatha and his family. Mistah publicly disgraced Abu Bakr. After the revelation of verses 11-21 of Surah Nour proving her innocence, Abu Bakr swore that he would no longer support Mistah bin Uthatha. Then verse 22 of Surah Noor was revealed: 'Let not those among you who are blessed with graces and wealth swear not to give (any sort of help) to their kinsmen, Al-Masakin (the poor), and those who left their homes for God's Cause. Let them pardon and forgive. Do you not love that God should forgive you? And God is Oft-Forgiving, Most Merciful.'

When he heard this verse, Abu Bakr said: "By God! We do want that God should forgive us." And he started helping Mistah more than before. Other companions who swore not to help the slanderers also revoked their oaths.

Even though jealous of each other, other wives did not participate in spreading the rumor. Ayisha said: "Zainab among the wives of the Holy Prophet was my strongest rival, but when in connection with the incident of the slander, the Holy Prophet asked her opinion of me, she said, `O Messenger of God, I swear by God that I have perceived nothing in her except piety'."

This incident led to creation of many principles of Islamic law.
"Why did they not produce four witnesses? Since the slanderers have not produced witnesses, they became liars before God."
That means, all dealings must be based on `good faith'. A bad opinion should be formed only on the basis of concrete evidence. Everybody should be considered innocent until proven guilty. Everybody should be considered truthful unless there are strong proof to the contrary.
Thus, the legal principle, 'one is innocent until proven guilty', was introduced for the first time in history. Later this principle was copied into law by many modern societies.

And why did you not, when you heard it, say: "It is not right for us to speak of this. Praise be to You O God! This is a great lie."
It was a grave sin to doubt the innocence and purity of Ayisha, the mother of all believers.

For a month Prophet Mohammed was upset and would make inquiries from the maid-servant, from his other wives, and sometimes from Ali and Usamah. Maid servant said she has seen her falling asleep while grinding corn, because she was very young and exhausted from hard work. Ali said prophet should divorce her and marry another. Because of this Ayisha had displeasure against Ali and she did not standup to help Ali and Fatima to get the property of Fadak which Prophet Mohammed gifted them. The quarrel about Fadak resulted in the untimely death of Fatima and her unborn child. Ayisha also did not stand up for Ali to succeed Prophet Mohammed.

Prophet Mohammed sent Ali to kill Safwan. He was instructed to keep his eyes open. When Safwan saw Ali coming with a sword, he ran up a tree and Ali saw his exposed genitals. Ali realized he was a eunuch and could not have done any sexual activity with Ayisha and he was left alone.

For one month, he was doubtful of Ayisha and he even asked her to repent if it is all true. He asked everybody including servants for information. He even sent Ali to kill Safwan. He knew the truth onoy when God revealed it to him. This incient proved that Prophet Mohammed had no special knowledge or [powerts other than what God has revealed to him.

When Abu Ayyub Ansari's wife told him the rumors, he asked: "Mother of Ayyub, if you had been there in place of Ayisha, would you have done that?" She replied, "By God, I would never have done it." Ayyub then said, "Well, Ayisha is a much better woman than you. As for myself if I had been in place of Safwan, I could never have entertained such an evil thought and Safwan is a better Muslim than I."

---

3 JESUS DICTATE LETTERS TO THE CHURCHES IN SARDIS, PHILADELPHIA AND LAODICEANS (RV.3)

RV.3: 1-3 “Write to the angel of the church in Sardis: ‘the one who has the seven Spirits of God and the seven stars says: ‘I know your works. I know that you had a good name and you live on the basis of that old name. But you are as good as dead. Be vigilant and strengthen the things which are still not completely dead. Because I have not found your works perfect before God. Therefore, remember and hold on to what you have received and heard and repent. If you are not watchful, I will come on you as a thief, at an hour unknown to you.

[The creature tells the church to hold on to what they have received and heard. That means they did not have books of bible and they have not even heard the whole story of Jesus. They just believe in whatever little they heard from some visiting preacher or some piece of parchment they have seen.

When Jesus said he will come as a thief at an hour unknown to them, he was talking about the end of the world. Here the creature is talking about one church. If they don’t repent and become perfect in the eyes of the creature, it will come like a thief and do what? Kill them of course. So, this is a death threat.]

RV.3: 4 You have a few names even in Sardis which have not defiled their garments; and they are worthy and shall walk with me in white.

[The creature promises to take the unnamed few people to heaven. When they reach heaven they will be given white uniform. What is the need for this uniform? Is it because the place is cold and need some warm clothing? Or, is it because the angels want to cover their nakedness? Prophet Mohammed also talks about the souls getting white clothes in heaven.]

RV.3: 5 The one who overcomes, shall be given white clothes; and I will not remove his name from the book of life, but I will plead his name before my Father and his angels.

RV.3: 6 He who has an ear, let him hear what the Spirit says to the churches."

[Here the creature is telling us that those who enter heaven are clothed in white raiment. That is interesting. Prophet Mohammed said the souls that enter heaven will be given white clothes. But, God did not think it was necessary to cloth Adam and Eve until they sinned. In garden east of Eden, God also must have been naked beause they did not notice any difference between them and God except that he is a heavy-set older man making noise when he walked on earth. Is everybody in heaven clothed in white or only some special people like the members of that church? There are rivers and trees and fruits in heaven. Is it possible that there are cotton crops and some of the angels are engaged in making white clothes for all the people in Heaven?

The creature also said he will not delete the name from the book of life. So, he has access to that book and permission to delete names from the book. He also pleads in front of the Father and his Holy angels. The holy angels must be like a committee and must be a level above the creature.

At this point most Christian apologists would say, if it walks and kwaks like Jesus, this creature must be Jesus. But it is not. Jesus sent this creature to John to give a message of imminent end of the world.]

RV.3: 7-9 "Write to the angel of the church in Philadelphia: The one who is godly and truthful and has the key of David, the one who opens and no man shuts and shuts and no man opens, says:
I know your works. I have set before you an open door which no man can shut because you are small in number and you have kept my word and you have not denied my name. Beware, of those who say they are Jews, and are not, but do lie. I will make them of the synagogue of Satan. I will make them to come and worship before your feet and to know that I have loved you.

[Jesus told a heavenly creature to come and inform John to tell the small Christian congregation of Jews in Philadelphia, to watch out for people who say they are Jews but are not and only lying.

Who are these 'Jews who are not Jews but liars who belong to the synagogue of Satan'?

Real Jews are descendants of Judah, son of Jacob. Over the years, many people converted into the religion of Jews and circumcised and submitted to the rule of Levite Priests. Those converts are treated like real Jews by the community but they are not real Jews in the eye of God. Jews departed from the teachings of Moses and they followed the wicked, filthy Talmud. Jesus called the Jewish Priests, children of Satan, belonging to the synagogue of Satan and brood of vipers. Jesus cursed the evil and wicked Jewish priests who would cross seven seas to find a convert so that they can make him twice as evil as themselves.

In the 10th century AD, they went to Khazaria and converted some Khazari nomads of the steppes of Kazakhstan into Judaism. They migrated to Eastern Europe and became known as the European Jews. From there they migrated TO Europe and to USA. These so-called European Jews are not real Jews, they are converts and follow the filthy wicked Talmud and kabbalah and they belong to the Synagogue of Satan. In the true sense of the word, these European Jews are twice as wicked as the Jews who killed Jesus and Jews have been creating strife N havoc among the nations of the world ever since.

The warning to church of Philadelphia is still valid today.

Jesus assures the Christian congregations that he will make those fake Jews belong to the synagogue of Satan (devil-worshippers). Then, Jesus further promises to make them come and worship at the feet of the Christians to prove that Jesus loves the members of the church congregation.

A tree is known by its fruits. Let us see if this promise came true. Throughout history, Jews were the staunchest opponents of Jesus and

Mohammed. They crucified Jesus and poisoned Mohammed. They hate Jesus because Jesus came exclusively to save them from their corrupt and vulgar Talmudic ways and to bring them back to the teachings of Moses. Moses gave 613 rules. These were difficult to follow. So, they made a new book called Talmud to circumvent these teachings. Moses said it is an abomination to for a man to lay with another man (homosexual acts). Talmud said a man becomes a man when he is 9 or 12 years old depending on the definition of the society at that time. In modern America a boy becomes a man at the age of 18 years. So, Talmud said: 'homosexuality is permitted as long as one of the partners is under the age of maturity'. There is no minimum age; so pedophilia was legitimate according to Talmud. Talmud encouraged its members to marry three year old Jewish girls and non-Jewish girls from day of birth onwards, and rape them regularly. Minimum age limit of three years applied only to Jewish girls. So it was legitimate for Jewish rabbis to rape regularly children from the time of birth. Thus, Talmud turned the Mosaic prohibition of homosexuality on its head and legitimized and encouraged the homosexuality with underage partners and pedophilia and rape of girls from time of birth without limit. Homosexuality and pedophilia are rampant among Jews even today. In similar fashion Talmud turned every Mosaic Law on its head. Jesus quoted one such instance. Moses said one must respect and help one's parents. Talmud said it is legitimate to ignore poverty stricken parents who are in need if that money was promised to the synagogue. Jews did not want to go back to the Mosaic rules which were difficult to practice and they wanted to continue practicing easy sensual corrupt vulgar Talmudic rules. So, they hated Jesus. They killed Jesus and persecuted those who believed in Jesus. Even today, the persecutions of Christians continue. Jews have infiltrated the Christian churches and corrupted the scriptures and spread false and corrupt teachings. In Israel, they have destroyed over 1600 ancient Christian churches and burned all copies of Christian bible and confiscated the land and property of the Christians and Muslims and killed millions of Christians and Muslims. In 2016, the chief rabbi has proclaimed that non-Jews should not be allowed to live in Israel. In modern times, Jews who control the American government makes America attack and destroy non-Jewish communities throughout the world under various pretexts.

Jesus promised to tackle the Jews immediately and make them worship at the feet of Christians. In 2000 years that promise did not come true; in fact just the opposite has happened. But, then again, for God 2000 years is like a day.]

RV.3: 10 Since you have kept the word of my patience, I will keep you from the hour of temptation, which shall come upon all the world to test those who live on earth.

[To this date, nobody knows what is: 'the word of my patience'. So, Jesus promised to protect the members of the church of Philadelphia from the world-wide temptation that is scheduled to come soon (in the lifetime of the members of the church). This temptation is to test everybody. No such worldwide temptation came in the last 2000 years. Usually when Jesus talks about the whole world he was only referring to the Palestine area. The Kito's wars were the only calamity that came upon the Jews after the revelation.]

RV.3: 11 I come quickly. Hold on to that which you have, so that no man takes your crown.

[This promise of quick second coming did not materialize and people are still waiting after 2000 years. But, for God 2000 years is like a day.]

RV.3: 12-13 I will make the one who overcomes, a pillar in the temple of my God. He shall not go out any more. I will write on him the name of my God and the name of the city of my God which is New Jerusalem that comes down out of heaven from my God and my new name. Let those who have an ear hear what the Spirit says to the churches.

[The creature's god has a temple. Pillars of that temple will be replaced by Church members who have overcome adversities. The creature will write God's name and 'New Jerusalem' and creatures' new name on these new human pillars. This is supposed to be a great honor.]

RV.3: 14 Write to the angel of the church in Laodiceans: ‘the Amen, the faithful and true witness, the first creation of God says:

[Here, the creature poked a big hole in the Paulian theory that Jesus is God. The creature says that he is the first creation of God. Anything that is created is not God.]

RV.3: 15-17 I know your works. You are neither cold nor hot. I would rather you were either cold or hot. I will spew you out of my mouth because you are lukewarm and because you say: ‘I am rich and gained more goods and have need of nothing’ and do not know that you are wretched, miserable, poor, blind and naked.

RV.3: 18-20 I recommend that you buy from me fire-tested gold so that you may be rich; and white garments so that you may be clothed and your shameful nakedness covered; and clean your eyes with eye ointment so that you may see. I rebuke and chasten those whom I love. Therefore, be motivated and repent. I stand at the door and knock. If anybody hear my voice and open the door, I will come in and will have supper with him and he with me.

RV.3: 21-22 I will grant him who overcomes to sit with me in my throne, just as I also overcame, and am set down with my Father in his throne. He who has an ear what the Spirit says to the churches.

[Here, the creature says, he faced adversities and he overcame them. And his father in heaven rewarded him by setting him on his throne. So, the creature attained such a high position by overcoming adversities. Are these the words of the creature or of Jesus?

If the creature is merely conveying the words of Jesus, then that means, Jesus attained his position by overcoming adversities. So, the Paulian theory that Jesus is God and he was around since before the creation of earth etc. is false.

Now, Jesus is promising to put on the throne anyone from this church group who overcomes adversities.

Anti-Christian New-Wave Cults created by Zionists and Freemasons, for example Jehovah's witness and Mormons and Seventh day Adventists, teach that Jesus is not God and that he is only an exalted human being and anybody can attain same position as Jesus by doing the right thing. Obeying the teachings of Jesus and Moses is not enough. Joining Freemasonry and propagating Zionism will help.

Isn't it interesting that members of different churches receive different rewards for overcoming adversities? Jesus, when he was alive told the story of laborers who came in at different hours of day and got the same reward.]

.

.

.

.

.

.

.

.

.

.

.

.

.

.

The Concept of Soul.

In Christian theology, the concept of soul is murky. Human body is a temporary house for the soul, during its earthly tour of duty. Souls are of unknown origin. We do not know where they come from. Many Christians believe that Souls are angels from heaven. Bible does not say souls are angels. Bible talks about different kinds of heavenly creatures like cherubim which look like young girls with wings, upon which god ride. Angels are male creatures with free will and usually work as soldiers under the leadership of Arch angels with Hebrew names like Michael and Gabriel. In addition to the army duty, they are employed as messengers. Bible does not talk about a category of heavenly creatures called souls. So where do they come from?

Scientists have discovered that when a sperm enters an egg, at that moment of fertilization, the egg emits light (fluorescence) acknowledging the birth of a new life. (Scientific Reports 6, Article number: 24737 (2016) doi:10.1038/srep24737). May be the soul is created at that moment of creation, or the soul enters the fertilized egg at that moment. Anyway, the soul sits around while the baby grows into adulthood. The soul does not seem to have any influence on the human body. After death, the body disintegrates into components and goes back to earth. Jesus said, fear God who can kill the body and throw the soul into eternal fire. (Mt. 10:28) So, body and soul are separate entities. They are together while the body is alive. The soul separates from body at moment of death. The Bible says Jesus gave up the ghost. That means, his soul came out of the body.

Jesus said: "Marvel not at this: for the hour is coming, in the which all that are in the graves shall hear his voice, and shall come forth; they that have done good, unto the resurrection of life; and they that have done evil, unto the resurrection of damnation." (John 5:28-29) So, may be the soul remain with the body and disintegrate into the earth. On the day of judgment, God will call all dead souls and they shall resurrect and face judgment. Those who were good go to heaven and others go to eternal fire. God judges the soul based on what the body did while it was alive.

How can the soul be judged for the actions of a body, on which it had no control or influence? In horse races, people bet on certain horse, let us say 'Black Queen'. Then the person who bet on it gets prize money or loses his bet based on the actions of the horse 'Black Queen'. The gambler simply bet on a name on the board. He has never seen the horse or raised the horse or trained the horse or know anything about the horse. He bet on a word written on a board. Then he was told the horse did badly and he lost his money or the horse did well and he got the prize. In this case, at least the gambler consciously selected a word written on the board. In the case of soul, did it choose the body to go into? The soul had no say in selecting the body and it had no influence on the actions of the body. Then at end of the game, God gives out the prize or put it in hell for ever. The 'burning in hell for eternity' part seems a bit harsh. The whole universe is God's horse racing game. He sets the rules. In the mind of God, the rules are just.

The OT told people to obey the commandments. If they obey, then god will reward them with more wives and children and goats. If they do not obey, they may lose wives and children and goats and god may not give rain on their two acres of land and their crops may fail and they may die of starvation. The reward and punishment are limited to this world and during the lifetime of the body. It was a simple concept.

Then, God sent Jesus. He changed everything. He moved the reward and punishment regime to a future time after death. He said his kingdom is not of this world; it is in heaven. People have to lose their bodies on earth to enter his kingdom. Based on the actions of the body on earth, the corresponding soul may enter the kingdom or be thrown into eternal fire.

In the OT, people could see with their own eyes the blessings and punishment of God. In the NT nobody can see the blessing or punishment. It all happens in a different realm.

"Jesus answered and said unto them, Ye do err, not knowing the scriptures, nor the power of God. For in the resurrection they neither marry, nor are given in marriage, but are as the angels of God in heaven. But as touching the resurrection of the dead, have ye not read that which was spoken unto you by God, saying, I am the God of Abraham, and the God of Isaac, and the God of Jacob? God is not the God of the dead, but of the living." (MT.22:29-32)

That means, people become like angels of God, after death, but they do not become angels. In America immigrant green-card-holders and citizens live the same way. The immigrants are like citizens but they are not citizens. Citizens vote and immigrants do not vote. Similarly, the souls of dead people are like angles, but are not angels.

Jesus said Abraham and Isaaac and Jacob are alive in heaven though their bodies were rotting in earth. So, may be the souls go to heaven immediately after death; before the final judgment. Jesus also told us the story of Lazarus. But that is only a story to drive home a moral lesson. It may not be literally true. May some good souls go to heaven immediately after death, while the average souls wait in grave until called up on day of judgment.

Souls are burned for eternity for the actions of some 'body' that lived and died on earth, over which the souls had no influence or control. Only god can justify such cosmic injustice.

People are told to obey the commandments, so that some souls which they have never seen or had any contact of any sort with, can go to heaven. Why would anybody do anything to make some imaginary thing happen to some imaginary entity after their death? If an imaginary entity that you have no connection with goes to hell, after you die, how does it bother you? It does not. The dead body is dead and gone. Preachers are scaring people with fire and brimstone as is if it is all going to happen to their body. They have no basis to make such threats. Since all souls are spiritual creatures, they have no shape or name or physical bodies. Eventually god will put a bunch of spiritual creations of his, in a lake of eternal fire. It is his game and his entertainment. Let it be. It has nothing to do with human beings or living bodies. So nobody should care about what happens after death. That is the logical conclusion of Christian theology.

Now, the Muslims have a different take on all these. " And they ask you, [O Muhammad], about the soul. Say, "The soul is of the affair of my Lord. And mankind have not been given of knowledge except a little." (Quran, Al-Israa (17: 85)) Or, in other words, God does not want us to know about it.

According to Prophet Mohammed, when a human being has completed 120 days in the womb of the mother, an angel of life visits him and gives him a soul. Souls were heavenly creatures. God has a reservoir full of them. Those souls who want to be born as human beings are given death and then a new birth in human body.

"He who created death and life to test you as to which of you is best in deed - and He is the Exalted in Might, the Forgiving" (Quran, Al-Mulk (67:2)). The word death is before birth. That means the soul was given death in heaven before being born into this world.

Then they will die again a second death and their souls are separated from their human body. Then the human body is brought back to life a second time and the soul is put back into the body, on the day of judgment.

" We said, "Go down from it, all of you. And when guidance comes to you from Me, whoever follows My guidance - there will be no fear concerning them, nor will they grieve. And those who disbelieve and deny Our signs - those will be companions of the Fire; they will abide therein eternally." (Quran, Al-Baqarah (2:38-39)).

Human life is a test. Those who pass the test, will enter heaven; others will be thrown into eternal fire.

God knows what will happen to these souls before they were put into a body. "No misfortune can happen on earth or to your soul but it is written in a decree before We bring it into existence. That is truly easy for God. In order that you may not despair over matters that pass you by, nor exult in favors bestowed upon you, for Allah loves not the vain boasters." (Quran, Al Hadid (57: 22-23))

Or, in other words, the free will, and just punishment for one's actions etc. are all a farce. In the end, those whom God has marked for hell will be thrown in hell fire.

"And truly, We did create man from a quintessence (of clay). Then We placed him (as a drop of sperm) in a place of rest, firmly fixed. Then We made the sperm into a clot of congealed blood. Then of that clot We made a (fetus) lump. Then We made out of that lump bones and clothed the bones with flesh. Then We developed out of it another creature (by breathing life into it). So blessed be God, the most marvelous Creator" (Quran, Al-Muminun (12:13-14)).

"Truly, the creation of each one of you is brought together in his mother's womb for forty days in the form of a nutfah (a thick clot of blood), then he becomes an 'alaqah (leech like stage) for a like period, then a mudghah (in the shape of a chewed substance) for a like period, then there is sent to him the angel who blows his soul into him and who is commanded with four matters: to write down his rizq (sustenance), his life span, his actions, and whether he will be blessed or wretched (whether he will enter Paradise or Hell).

Truly one of you performs the actions deserving Paradise until he is close to it by an arm's length, and that which has been written overtakes him, and so he acts as if he deserves Hellfire and he enters it; and truly, one of you performs actions deserving Hellfire, until there is but an arm's length between him and it, and that which has been written overtakes him and so he acts like deserving Paradise and thus he enters it. (Sahih Bukhari, Hadith: 3208, 2898; Sahih Muslim, Hadith: 2643)"

That is an interesting concept. The fate of a human being is unchangeably determined 120 days after conception. A person may act all his life as if he deserves Hell but when he get very close to Hell, what was written about him overtakes him and he does something deserving heaven and he enters heaven. A person may act all his life as if he deserves Paradise, but when he is near it, what was written about him overtakes him and he does something deserving Hell and he enters hell. Or, in other words, when the angel blow the soul into the child he also writes his sustenance (how he is going to earn his livelihood), his time of death, his actions during his life and his final destination (whether he will enter heaven or hell). There is nothing anybody can do to change this writing. The fate will take over in the last minute. If everything is predetermined in the womb, what is the purpose of all these fasting and prayers? God saves whom he chooses and God destroys whom he pleases.

NOTE: Muslims consider killing a fetus after 120 days, is murder. A 120 day old fetus should be buried like an adult. "... if anyone killed a person not in retaliation of murder, or (and) to spread mischief in the land — it would be as if he killed all mankind, and if anyone saved a life, it would be as if he saved the life of all mankind..." (Quran, Al-Maidah, (5:32)).

The child grows to adulthood. He is supposed to praise God and do good deeds. After death, his body will be still aware of the environment. He can hear and see but he cannot respond. After the body is placed in the grave, after people leave, there will be a judgment of his actions. The walls of grave will come together and squeeze him. That is the terror in the grave. This will be horrifying experience. Now, if the soul has already departed the body, this is happening to the physical body, not to the soul.

Prophet Mohammed told people that the eyes follow the departing soul. So, he advised people to close the eyes of the dead. According to Prophet Mohammed, the souls depart from the body. Where do they go? Then the soul will be brought back to the body and subjected to the terror of the grave!(?).

"Every soul shall taste death, and only on the Day of Judgement will you receive your full compensation. The one who is saved from the Fire and admitted into Paradise will have attained success. And what is the life of this world except the enjoyment of delusion" (Quran, Ali Imran (3:185)).

Prophet Mohammed used to pray everyday like this: "My Lord, I seek refuge in You from the punishment of the grave, and seek refuge in You from the torture of the hell fire, and I seek refuge in You from the trials of the false messiah, and I seek refuge in You from the trials of living and dying."

Zaid bin Thabit narrated how, when the Prophet and his Companions were once passing some graves of polytheists, the Prophet's horse bolted and almost unseated him. The Prophet explained: "These people are being tortured in their graves, and were it not that you would stop burying your dead, I would ask Allah to let you hear the punishment in the grave which I can hear." (Sahih Muslim)
Please Note: Punishment in the grave is not mentioned in Quran.

At the end of the world, all creatures that ever lived on earth will be brought back to life again in their best form. Then all those bodies will stand on a flattened earth without sun or moon for 50000 years while the process of judgment takes place. All the animals that were unnecessarily cruel to other animals, for example, the goats that had horns against sheep without horns, etc. will be avenged . Then all animals and creatures will be turned to dust. Then souls who have been judged 'good' will be allowed to proceed to heaven in their physical bodies. The souls who were judged 'bad' will be thrown into eternal fire in their physical bodies. And those who go to heaven will live there, eating fruits and drinking water and peeing and pooping wherever possible, for eternity.

In Muslim theology, it is the physical body that does good or bad and it is the re-constituted physical body that is rewarded or punished.

When the "Prophet Mohammed, explained resurrection to the pagans, a

Bedouin by the name of Ubayy bint Khalaf picked up a decayed bone and crumbled it to dust and then asked: "Who will restore to life the scattered particles of this rotten bone?" The answer was in the verse: "(O Mohammed) say: `God Who first brought them to life will restore them to life. He has knowledge of all His creation.' ... Isn't He who created the heavens and the earth capable of creating the likes of them? Yes, he is. He is the all Knowing Creator. When he intent to create a thing, he only commands to it 'Be' and it is. He, in whose hand is the realm of all things, is exalted and to Him you will be returned." (Quran, Ya Sin (36: 79, 81-83)) "

Quran talked about the importance and uniqueness of finger prints, 1300 years before scientists found out that the finger print of each person is unique. Quran says, on the day of judgement, everybody will be recreated exactly as they were. Even the very finger tips (with their unique finger prints) would be in perfect order.
"Does man think that We(God) cannot assemble his bones? Nay, We are able to put together in perfect order, the very tip of his fingers." (Quran, Al Qiyamah (75:3-4))

At the time of Prophet Mohammed nobody knew about the finger prints or the importance of finger tips in positive identification. No two finger prints are alike. They are like the serial number stamped on the product, from the factory. So, in the Muslim theology, every human being has a responsibility to do good because it is their own flesh which will be rewarded or tormented. Soul is a part of the physical body.

In Hundu theology, the bodies are disintegrated by fire or by burial. The spirit that was a part of the body will be borm again as some other creature. The cycle of brith and rebirths will continue until a perfect life will make the soul eligible to become one with the creator. The spirit that is part of body will have the same shape but not mass or weight. It will be like holographic image until it takes birth as another creature.

---

4 JOHN LIFTED TO HEAVEN TO SEE THE FUTURE (RV.4)

RV.4: 1 After this, a door was opened in heaven: and a trumpet-like voice told me: 'Come up here, and I will show you things which must happen in the future'.

[If Jesus was planning to lift John up to heaven anyway, why did he send a strange creature to dictate letters to the churches?]

RV.4: 2-11 Immediately I was filled with the spirit. A throne was set in heaven, and one who looked like a 'jasper and sardine' stone sat on the throne. The throne which resembled an emerald was surrounded by a rainbow. Twenty four elders wearing white clothes and gold crowns sat on seats placed around the throne. Lightnings and thunders and voices came out of the throne. In front of the throne, the seven Spirits of God stood in the form of seven lamps of fire. In front of the throne was a sea of crystal glass. In the middle of the throne and around the throne stood four beasts with six wings and full of eyes before and behind and within. The first beast rrsembled a lion, the second beast resembled a calf, the third beast had a man's face, and the fourth beast resembled flying eagle.

They continually say: 'Godly, godly, godly, Master, God Almighty, which was, and is, and is to come.'

Then the beasts gave praise and honor and thanks to the immortal who sat on the throne. The twenty four elders threw their crowns before the throne and fell down before the immortal and worshipped him saying: 'you are worthy, O God, to receive glory and honour and power because <u>you have created all things and they were and are created for your pleasure</u>.'

[The imagery of lightning, thunder and sounds shooting out of the seat of God is from the Old Testament. However John describes much more than the OT.

A lot of hallucinogenic plants grew on Patmos Island. John must have ingested some of those plants and started hallucinating. The psychedelic visions described here are similar to those that happen after ingesting LSD. Native American 'Shamans' (medicine men) use peyote, a hallucinogen, in their religious rituals. Peyote is a cactus containing 'mescaline'. For thousands of years, Native Americans have used to create psychedelic experiences which they consider divine revelations. They sit in a circle inside a tepee and drink tea made from peyote and smoke tobacco, cedar and sage. The bitter, foul-tasting peyote tea induces vomiting which is considered part of cleansing. It also produces incredible, brilliantly colored visions and spiritual experiences.]

.

.

.

.

.

.

.

.

.

.

.

.

.

.

.

.

5 BOOK WITH SEVEN SEALS, LAMB WITH SEVEN HORNS TAKES THE BOOK TO READ (RV.5)

RV.5: 1 I saw a book written within and on the backside, sealed with seven seals, in the right hand of him who sat on the throne.

[John does not tell us who is sitting on the throne. He wants to keep us guessing. The man on the throne is holding a book with seven seals. In those days, book meant a scroll. Seven seals is like multiple padlocks. Breaaking of each of the seals is a big event. What kind of a book is it? Why is it sealed? Who put the seals on the book? Why seven seals? Who and why the seals were set up to create havoc on earth when it is broken? The seals will be broke, but the book will never be opened or read. If the book is not going to be read or written to, why break the seals? Why would Dorothy follow yellow brick road instead of pink brick road in wizard of OZ? Who shot JR, in the TV series of the 70's Dallas? There is no rhyme or reason to any of this. It is all simple drama.

John is making a big deal about 'seven'. Seven this, seven that, seven everything and seven everywhere. That is because he was writing to seven Christian congregations. A similar situation is seen in the books of Moses. Moses was preoccupied with 12. 12 tribes, 12 stones, 12 this and 12 that. According to John, God and Jesus are preoccupied with these seven small Asian congregations of Jews who believed in Jesus.]

RV.5: 2-3 I saw a well-built angel asking in a loud voice: 'Who is worthy to open the book, and to loose its seals?' No man in heaven, or in earth, or under the earth was able to open the book or to look on it.

[The angel who is asking the inhabitants of heaven, earth and under-world is a well-built angel. Either he exercises regularly and have built up a six pack or he is a superior Greek or Roman angel. Looks matter in heaven.

Jesus told John to come up and see the future events. He is supposed to see what is to come and then write it all in a book (and make seven copies and send it to seven churches). John says no man in heaven or on earth or below earth was able to look at the book or open it. So, the angel asked in a loud voice and people in the three layers of the universe (heaven, earth and hell) heard it. They understood what the angel was referring to and they could not even look at the book or open it. So, all three worlds have become transparent layers. The people who live in the underworld could see through the layer of earth where living humans live and see all the way through the floor of the heaven and see and hear everything that is happening in heaven. They could perhaps see the immortal man who is sitting on the throne. Everybody understood what angel was shouting about: because everybody in heaven, hell and earth understands Greek language. (God spoke Hebrew. Jesus spoke Aramaic. But everybody everywhere learned Greek in a hurry so that John, who speaks Greek can understand.) This event is happening in the not-so-distant future at end of the world.

Muslims talk about end of the world and final judgment. All living creatures who ever lived will be brought back to life and they will all stand on earth, packed like matchsticks in a matchbox. God has already flattened the earth and spread it out so that all creatures could fit in it. They would stand there naked for very long time, 50 thousand years, while they are all judged. In John's vision everybody in heaven is wearing white Egyptian cotton Togas.]

RV.5: 4-6 I cried a lot because no man was found worthy to open and to read the book or to even look at it. One of the elders told me: 'Don't cry. Look, the Lion of the tribe of Juda, the Root of David, has succeeded in opening the book, and to loose its seven seals.' Then, I saw a slain Lamb with seven horns and seven eyes, which are the seven Spirits of God sent into all the earth. It stood in the middle of the throne among the four beasts and the elders.

[Is John in heaven standing next to Jesus or is he still on Patmos Island smoking peyote? When Jesus invited him up, he was filled with the spirit. But did he literally ascend to heaven? He talked to one of the elders sitting around Jesus. So, John is literally in heaven. It is nice to have friends in high places.

This whole heaven appears to be a drama stage. Who are those people below the earth? John was talking about people in the underworld or Hades from Greek mythology. Underworld, in Christian mythology, is a lake of fire and brimstone and people there are in pain and they are not listening to what an angel says in heaven.

John is watching all this future drama. He counted 24 men and they looked the 'Elder' type. Elders mean senior members, not necessarily old men, of the community. Are these the senior members of the heavenly community?

How big is the throne? In the middle of the throne there is a beast covered with eyes, and a slain sheep with seven horns. Where is the immortal man sitting? In one corner? How did John know that he is immortal? Did he look like the immortal type? So far the immoral man has not spoken a word. These are details an observer will not know, but a fiction writer would know.]

RV.5: 7-10 And he came and took the book out of the right hand of the man who sat on the throne. Then the four beasts and twenty four elders fell down before the Lamb. Every one of them had harp and golden vials full of odours, which are the prayers of saints. They sung a new song: 'you are worthy to take the book, and to open its seals because you were slain, and have redeemed us to God by your blood out of every kindred, and tongue, and people, and nation; and have made us to our God kings and priests: and we shall reign on the earth.'

[The root of David, which is Jesus, came and took the book from the hand of the man on the throne. So, the man on the throne was not Jesus. The mystery thickens. At this point John made this drama into a musical. Everybody (including the beasts) fell down before the lamb. While lying in that position they pulled out their pocket harps and played and sang a new song. How did John know it is a new (never before sung) song? Heavenly creatures can play harps lying down.

For 2000 years, experts have tried to interpret all this in a cohesive manner and failed. But we have to believe that all this has some very deep meaning; something ordinary mortal would not understand. If nobody understands it, why even write it? It is perhaps like the encrypted message on the sculpture in front of the CIA headquarters, which no one can decipher.]

RV.5: 11-12 I saw and heard the loud voice of large crowds of angels around the throne, and the beasts and the elders: 'the slain Lamb is worthy to receive power, riches, wisdom, strength, honour, fame and blessing.'

[John tells us that the lamb deserve to receive power and riches and wisdom and strength and honor and fame and blessing, because it was slain. Obviously, it did not have these things before. We are not sure what kind of power did the lamb attain: political, physical, mental, financial or some other kind? He also received riches. Where will a slain lamb with seven horns spend his riches? The Lamb received blessing. Who blessed the lamb? John did not tell us. Maybe he did not think through all these before writing. Perhaps it is a mystery like the 'trinity' and the reader is supposed to accept it without questioning.

When Jesus spoke parables, his audience did not understand it immediately. But most of it were understood later. Parables were stories with a moral. Here, John is not telling a story, it is supposed to be understood, but nobody understands it even after 2000 years.]

RV.5: 13-14 I heard every creature which is in heaven, and on the earth, and under the earth, and in the sea, saying: 'Let Blessing and honor and fame and power be upon the one who sits on the throne and the Lamb, for ever and ever.' And the four beasts said, 'Amen'. And the twenty four elders fell down and worshipped the immortal man sitting on the throne.

[The one sitting on the throne is immortal. That means others on the stage are mortals. So, according to John, those who inhabit heavens will die one day.
There is a solid floor to the heavens and there is gravity. Otherwise the twenty four Elders cannot fall down. Perhaps, heaven is above earth and

is subject to the earth's gravity.

According to John, creatures live in heaven, on earth, under the earth and in sea. So, sea is separate from the three worlds. Also, creatures in all these worlds can speak and they speak the language of the author. John is Greek. He doesnot know any other language. So, if John heard and understood what the angels and elders were saying, they must have been speaking Greek. That means the language of heaven is Greek.]

.

.

.

.

.

.

.

.

.

.

.

.

.

.

.

.

Mathematical Miracles in Quran

They said, "Why hasn't a miracle come down to him from his God?" Say, "Only God knows the future. Therefore, wait, and I will wait along with you." (Quran (10:20))

Those who disbelieved said, "This is no more than a fabrication by him, with the help of other people." Indeed, they uttered a blasphemy; a falsehood. Others said, "Tales from the past that he wrote down; they were dictated to him day and night." Say, "This was sent down from the One who knows `the secret' in the heavens and the earth." Surely, He is Forgiving, Most Merciful. (Quran (25:4-6)).

In Quran, man and woman are considered equal. The words 'man' and 'woman' occur 24 times each.
In Quran, Satan is an angel who is permitted to test humans. The words 'Satan' and 'Angel' occur 68 times each.
Quran says the life continues after death. The words 'this life' and 'next life' occur 115 times each.

The word 'month' occurs 12 times.
At the time of prophet Mohammed , people used lunar calendar. Lunar year had only 360 days. Yet, the word 'day' occurs 365 times.
There are too many of these word patterns to have occurred by chance.

It could not have been by human design because these patterns came to light only in the second half of 20-th century, through analysis using computers. So, it has to be by divine design.

The Quran was recited to Prophet Mohammed by angel Gabriel, verse by verse over a 23 year period, often in response to new and unexpected events. It would be inconceivable to remember how many times he mentioned a particcular word like 'day' or 'angel' over a period of 23 years. The number of days in a year at his time was 360. But the word occurs 365 times. Julian calendar with 365 days was introduced centuries later.
So, the Quran must have been designed that way by divine power who knew the earth moves around the sun in 365 days , not 360 days.

During the life time of Prophet Moahmmed, thousands and thousands of Muslims have memorized all or large portions of the Quran. Quran was recited from memory in a continuous stream. The verses were not separated. They did not know how many verses a particular chapter contained. Later when Quran was written down, the scribes, over centuries, separated verses and then numbered the verses and chapters. Thus, no human author decided that a certain chapter should have a certain number of verses. Yet, in the modern times, computer analysis has shown many instances of surprising relationships between numbers of chapters, verses, words, and letters in the Quran.

Chapter 57 'Iron' has 29 verses.
57 x 29 = 1653
The sum of 1 to 57 is the same:
1+2+3+. . .+ 57=1653
The numbers of verses were carefully chosen to bring about this relationship.

The chapter 22 'The Pilgrimage' has the Quran's last mention of 'pilgrimage'. It is in verse number 27. This verse has 14 words.
14 x 27 = 378
1+2+3+. . .+ 27=378
The number of words in this verse was carefully chosen to bring about this correspondence.

The chapter 71 'Noah' has 28 verses.
Also, there are 28 different chapters that mention Noah.
Some chapters mention Noah more than once. Noah is mentioned a total of 43 times.
43+28=71
43+71=114 which is the total number of chapters in the Quran.
28 chapters mention Noah, and 86 chapters do not mention Noah, which is 43 x 2.
The last mention of Noah is in the chapter of Noah. Of the 86 chapters that do not mention Noah, 43 come before the chapter of Noah and 43 chapters come after it.
Thus chapter 71 'Noah' is strategically placed and its number of verses is carefully chosen to bring about these complex relationships.

The chapter 13 'Thunder'. The word 'thunder' occurs in verse number 13. This verse also, coincidentally, occurs in the 13th part of the Quran. Quran has 114 chapters of unequal length. The Quran is divided into 30 parts of roughly equal length so that reading of one part each day will complete the book in a month. The 13-th verse of the 13-th chapter occurs in the 13th part.
The same verse has 19 words. These words are written with 83 letters. There is one other place in the entire Quran that mentions 'thunder'. That is chapter 2, verse number 19. This verse also has 19 words written with 83 letters, although the words are mostly different. No human being could have produced such correspondences. It points to a divine hand in the creation of Quran.

Chapter 32 is called 'Prostration' because it mentions the key word 'sujjadan' (prostrate). As is typical of the Arabic language, this word is derived from the three-letter root SJD to which vowels and other increments are used to produce a variety of words clustered around the root meaning "to prostrate."
Words based on this root are used in 32 different chapters of the Quran. The chapter number with this name is also 32.

The verse in this chapter which mentions prostration is such that a believer naturally wants to prostrate to God after reading it. Now, in the entire Quran there are 15 such verses which have been traditionally noted as 'verses of prostration'.
The number of verses in this chapter is 30. Half of that number is 15. The 15-th verse has the 'prostration' in chapter 32 ('Prostration').

There are 372 words in this chapter.
372 / 2 = 186.
The key word 'Prostration' is the 186-th word in this chapter.

Chapter 27 'The Ant' has 93 verses. It begins with two mysterious letters which correspond roughly to the English letters T and S. These two initials do not spell a word. It has been believed until now that God has placed such initials in the beginning of each chapter but nobody , including prophet Mohammed , knew what was its meaning. Modern computer analysis has shown that in chapter 27 the letter T is written 27 times.

In this same chapter, consisting of 93 verses, the letter S is written 93 times.
It seems that this correspondence was planned. It would be impossible for a human being to arrange it this way.
If a human being had arranged verses according to some formula, the author would have told others about this miraculous feature.

Every chapter of the Quran except chapter 9 begins with the familiar phrase "In the Name of God, Most Gracious, Most Merciful." On the other hand, chapter 27 is the only chapter that mentions the phrase in the body of the chapter. Hence, one reading the chapters sequentially is initially surprised to find it absent from the beginning of chapter 9 and again present in the body of chapter 27.
There is a numerical relationship between these two chapters.
The difference between the chapter numbers is 27-9=18.
The number of chapters from 9 to 27 inclusive is 19.
These two results, 18 and 19, form an interesting relationship with the chapter numbers of these two chapters. Consider:
18 x 19 = 342
9+10+11+ . . . +27 = 342
In chapter 27 we have the only verse in the Quran to mention the word 'ant.' The verse number is 18 and it contains 19 words. That is another relation between 18 and 19.

Complex mathematical relationships between chapter and verse numbers have been found. An error check bit is built into the Quran to assure us that its chapter and verses were transmitted without error, and that the Quran is of divine origin.
Chapters are sequentially numbered and therefore chapter numbers alternate between odd and even. 1 is odd, 2 is even, 3 is odd, etc.
The number of verses in each chapter are not sequentially ordered. If we add each chapter number to the number of verses in that chapter we get 114 separate numbers.

It is a miracle that 57 of these numbers are even numbers and 57 are odd numbers.
If we take the sum of all the even numbers, the result is 6236.
This sum is also the total number of verses in the entire Quran.
If we take the sum of all the odd numbers, the result is 6555.

This sum is also the sum of all the chapter numbers, i.e. 1+2+3+ . . . +114=6555

Total verses in each chapter and their chapter numbers together provide two check sums. If any alteration has been made to the original text, these numbers will not match. Quran also says it is a miracle in itself. We are only beginning to understand why Quran called itself a miracle. Quran has complex arrangements to guarantee its faultless preservation. This grand design points to its divine origin and its faithful preservation. Quran says the whole universe was designed by God with numbers. Modern scientists have discovered that the nature employs 'Virahanka' numbers of Indian mathematics or its western version the 'Fibonacci numbers' and 'Golden ratio' and 'Prime numbers' extensively in constructing our universe.
We are only beginning to understand the mathematical miracles hidden in Quran. The Hadiths (sayings of Prophet Mohammed) says in the last days a miracle in Quran will be discovered. What would that be?

---

6 FIRST SIX SEALS ARE OPNENED *(RV.6)*

RV.6: 1-2 When the Lamb opened the first seal, one of the four beasts said in thunderous voice: 'Come and see'. Then, I saw a man on a *white horse*, with a bow. A crown was given to him. He went forward conquering and to conquer.

[Note: Rev. 6 is similar to Mathew 24.
(Jesus) told John to come and see what is going to happen soon. The lamb, which again is Jesus, opened the first seal. A man on a horse with a bow was made king and he went forward conquering and to conquer. Who made him king? King of what? What exactly was he conquering? Nations? Or minds of people? Something else?

Many preachers assume that the first horseman is the leader who will conquer the whole world and establish the New World Order – one world, one government, one religion (Jewish)]

RV.6: 3-4 When he had opened the second seal, the second beast said: 'Come and see'. A man riding a *red horse* went out. Power was given to him to take peace from the earth, so that they should kill one another. A large sword was given to him.

[Then, the world will be thrust into political turmoil, wars, and social unrest and chaos.]

RV.6: 5-6 When he had opened the third seal, the third beast said: 'Come and see'. Then I saw a man on a *black horse* with a pair of balances in his hand. A voice in the middle of the four beasts said: 'a measure of wheat for a penny, and three measures of barley for a penny; and see you do not hurt the oil and the wine.'

[There will be famine and scarcity of food and price of food will rise. One Penny was the compensation for a 12 hour day's work, in those days.]

RV.6: 7-8 When he had opened the fourth seal, the fourth beast said: 'Come and see'. Then, I saw a *pale horse* and a man with name 'Death' riding it and Hell followed with him. They were given power to kill over fourth of the earth with sword, hunger, death and beasts of the earth.

[Quarter of the population will die by various means.]

RV.6: 9-10 When he had opened the fifth seal, I saw under the altar the souls of those who were slain for the word of God, and for the testimony which they held. They cried with loud voice: 'O godly and true Master, how long do you wait to judge and avenge our blood on those who live on the earth?'

[Those who were killed for believing in and professing Jesus were hiding under the altar. When the sixth seal on the book of life was broken, they came out like the goblins coming out of graves on Halloween night, and cried and asked how long will Master wait to judge their slayers. Generally Christians belive good men go to heaven right away after death. Here, we are told that the souls hide out somewhere in heaven until the end of the world when the sixth seal is broken.

Muslims believe the good souls are taken to heaven and the bad ones are tormented in grave after they are dead. The souls cannot officially enter as full fledged members until after judgment. Martyrs and assorted good ones are allowed to hang around the chandeliers of heaven. Both good and bad will be brought back to life on the judgment day. On thr judgment day, those who are found suitable to enter heaven will be given white coveralls. Prophet Mohammed will be the first to enter Heaven.

Anyway, these slain souls are asking Jesus to take revenge on their slayers even though Jesus taught everybody to forgive and forget.]

RV.6: 11 They were given white robes and told to rest for a little while longer until the killing of their fellow servants and their brethren that would be killed, are also accomplished.

[Who told the slain souls to rest for a little while longer until those who are scheduled to be slain like them also die and come to heaven, before the slayers are punished?

God has created some people to be slain for their faith. They are preordained to enter heaven as martyrs.

On one occasion, Ayisha told Prophet Mohammed about a child who died. Then, she asked if that child will surely go to heaven, because he hasn't done any sin? Prophet Mohammed answered that it was not guaranteed. Because god who created hell has also created people to go into it. Or, in other words, god will put in hell whom he wants and God will put in heaven whom he wants. Everything is predetermined when the child is still in the womb.]

RV.6: 12-17 When he had opened the sixth seal, I saw a great earthquake. *The sun became black as hair and the moon became as blood. The stars of heaven fell to the earth,* like figs fall when a fig tree is shaken by strong wind. The heaven went away like a scroll when it is rolled together. Every mountain and island were moved out of their places. People of earth hid themselves in the dens and in the rocks of the mountains and told the mountains and rocks: 'Fall on us, and hide us from the face of him who sits on the throne and from the wrath of the Lamb: because the great day of his wrath is come and who shall be able to stand it?'

[Rev. 6 is an illustrated version of Mathew 24.]

.

.

.

.

.

.

.

7 ANGELS STAMP SEAL OF LIVING GOD ON FOREHEADS OF 144000 JEWS, COUNTLESS SOULS SAVED (RV.7)

RV.7: 1-8 Then, I saw four angels standing on the four corners of the earth, holding back the four winds of the earth, from blowing on the earth or on the sea or on any tree. I saw another angel carrying the seal of the living God ascending from the east crying out to the four angels, who were to hurt the earth and the sea: 'Do not hurt the earth, or the sea, or the trees, till we have sealed the servants of our God in their foreheads. I heard hundred and forty four thousand of all the tribes of the children of Jacob, which is twelve thousand from each of the tribes, were sealed.

[Out of all the descendants of Jacob, only 144,000 were marked for protection. Preachers interpret this 144000 as representing all believers. 12 tribes started out of Egypt with Moses and settled in Palestine. Then, 10 of the tribes which settled in the north became the country called Israel and the two tribes of the south became the country of Judah. Syrians defeated the country of Israel and made it one of its provinces with capital in Samaria. The ten tribes were intermingled with Syrians and became known as Samaritans whom Jesus hated. Samaritans are the 10 lost tribes. When Jesus said he came to save the lost tribes, he did not mean Samaritans; he was talking about the 2 tribes that survived as 'Judah-ens' (or Jews) who deviated from Laws of Moses and followed the wicked and filthy Talmud and Kabbalah known to Jesus as 'the traditions of the elders'. So, the '144000 from 12 tribes' should not be taken literally. Then again, who are we to decide what should be taken literally and what should not be taken literally. John wrote the book, and if he did not want it to be taken literally, he would have said so.]

RV.7: 9-10 Then I saw a large crowd of countless number of people from all tribes and families and civilizations and languages stood before the throne and before the Lamb, wearing white robes and palm leaves in their hands. They cried out loudly: 'Salvation to our God who sits on the throne and to the Lamb.'

[Salvation to God who is sitting on the throne and to the lamb? God and Jesus were in need of salvation? And these people are giving salvation to God? Who are these people? Where did they get their white robes?]

RV.7: 11-12 All the angels who stood around the throne and the elders and the four beasts fell before the throne on their faces and worshipped God Saying: 'We agree that blessing, fame, wisdom, thanksgiving, honor, power and might be to our God for ever and ever. We agree.'

[So, the angels in heaven agreed and acknowledged that Blessing, and fame, and wisdom, and thanksgiving, and honor, and power, and might belong to God. Here, either the angels or the author is mocking god. God does not need their approval and acknowledgement for having wisdom.]

RV.7: 13-17 Then one of the Elders asked me: 'Who are these wearing white robes? And where did they come from?' I replied: 'Sir, you know'.

He told me: 'They are the ones who came out of great tribulation. They have washed their robes in the blood of the Lamb and made them white. Therefore they are before the throne of God and serve him day and night in his temple. He who sits on the throne shall live among them. They shall not hunger or thirst any more; neither shall the light and heat of the sun fall on them. Because the Lamb which is in the middle of the throne shall feed them and shall lead them to living fountains of waters and God shall wipe away all their tears.'

[These multitudes of people overcame the tribulaions in their lives and then they came up to heaven and washed their robes in the blood of the Lamb and made it white. In heaven blood of Lamb will not stain clothes but whiten them. Those who were slain had to wait until now to get their white robes. Those who overcame the tribulations brought their own robes and laundered it in heaven. But where did they get their palm leaves? The lamb feeds them and then leads them to the living fountains to drink from. If they are eating and drinking, the numerous souls will need large number of toilets. Hopefully heaven has a good sewer system.]

Embryology in Quran.

The 'International Journal of Health Sciences publishd by Qassim University, in its 2009 January edition, explained the Quranic descriptions of the development of Embryo in light of modern medical knowledge.

Aristotle thought that foetus was formed in uterus from a coagulum of blood and seed from menstrual blood. Greeks and Europeans thought that foetus was created from menstrual blood, or else they thought that foetus was fully created and was in a miniature form in sperm or in ovule. In 1604 Fabricus came out with excellent drawings of chicken embryo. Malphigi in 1672 who is considered father of modern embryology thought poultry eggs contained a miniature chicken and others thought that human being was fully formed in sperm or an ovum. He came out with chick drawings showing clear somites.

In 1673 Leeuwenhoek invented the first microscope. Hartsoeker's drawing of a human spermatozoon in 1694 clearly indicated that a fully formed human being was in a spermatozoon or in ovum. In 1775 Spallanzani showed the necessity of both ovum and sperm for the development of a new individual.

In 19th century, the development cycle of mammalian ovum was discovered. Starting 1940, sophisticated instruments were used for the study of the development of embryo.

Prophet Muhammad was illiterate, had no formal education and it was through him that Muslim scholars had the knowledge about conception, morphology, various phases of intrauterine life which modern day scientists came to know only recently.

In Quran there is reference of various stages of human enbryonic development in many chapters.

"We (God) created man from a quintessence of clay. We then placed him as a nutfah (drop) in a place of settlement, firmly fixed, then We made the drop into an alaqah (leech like structure), and then We changed the alaqah into a mudghah (chewed like substance),then We made out of that mudghah, izam (skeleton,bones),then We clothed the bones with lahm (muscles,flesh) then We caused him to grow and come in being and attain the definitive (human)form. So, blessed be God, the best to create." (Quran: Surah Al-Mu'minun,(23:12–14)).

These stages can be chronologically arranged as follows:

Nutfah amshaj (drop that is mixed): this stage covers the period from fertilization to implantation. Nutfa means a drop and amshaj means mixtures. This term describes the mixture and convergence of male and female fluids in the uterine or the Fallopian tubes to form zygote. It has the form of a drop of fluid and consists of a mixture of male and female secretions. This process of formation of a single individual by fusion of two secretions has been correctly described by the term 'Khalak'.

The human creation begins with formation of a zygote. The next phase is Taqdir according to Quran. Modern science calls it genetic programming. The Taqdeer in Arabic means planning, determining or programming. Taqdir is an accurate word to describe what happens. This process is completed within 30 hours after fertilization. The sex is determined in this phase.

"And He did create the two sexes, the male and the female from Nutfah when emitted or planned" (Quran: surah An-Najam, (53:45-46)). If sperm with a "Y" chromosome fertilizes ovum, it is a male child and if sperm with a "X" chromosome fertilizes ovum it is a female child.

When the phases of Khalk and Taqdir are completed, the zygote migrates from from fallopian tube to the uterus where it implants itself similar to a seed planting in soil. Quran accurately describes the zygote settling in a place of settlement. It gets embedded in endometrium and receives its nourishment and develops a different shape and structure. It is mentioned in Quran that endometrial lining of the uterus is similar to the

soil in which a seed is embedded.
"The Angel enters upon the conceptus (nutfah) after it rests in the uterus for forty or forty-five nights....(Hadith, Sahih Muslim).

The second main Stage of Embryonic development is **Takhliq (Creation).** It starts at the beginning of the third week upto eighth week and is a process of rapid cell growth and cell differentiation takes place to form systems and organs.

The embryo goes through the following stages:

In the **Alaqah** Phase (starts on day 15 and is completed on day23 or 24),

the embryo gradually acquires the shape of a leech, the Arabic word "alaqah" has three meanings --- (i) Leech (ii) a suspended thing (iii) a blood clot. There is a great similarity between a fresh water leech to early embryo.

The second meaning is a suspended thing and that is what we can see the way embryo is attached to the placenta in this stage. Both these meanings describe and reflect accurately the external appearance of embryo at this stage. The third meaning –"the blood clot" describes the most important internal structure that affects the external appearance, for in alaqah stage blood is formed in the blood vessels in the form of isolated islands and the embryo resembles a blood clot descriptions are given miraculously by a single word----"Alaqah".

From 24 to 26 days, The embryo changes from Alaqah to **Mudgaha** stage. The word Mudghahah means:

- Something that has been chewed by teeth
- A piece of a meat of a chewable size
- Small substance

In this phase the embryo resembles a chewed substance that still bears the teeth marks. The embryo shows the distinct somites which resemble teeth marks in the embryo's body. The second and the third meaning of

Mudghah apply to the embryo in relation to its size for it is approximately 1 centimeter in length, the size of a chewable object. Outside surface in Alaqah stage is smooth and in Mudghah stage, it acquires furrows, swellings and corrugated surface which gives the embryo the chewed appearance. The word Mudghah accurately describes the appearance of the embryo in this stage. The embryo stays in Mudgaha stage upto 6 weeks.

The next stage is the **izam (bones).** In the beginning of seventh week, cartiligenous skeleton begins to form and eventually the embryo takes the human shape with formation of skeleton. Until recently Embryologists believed that bones and muscles developed together. Quran accurately stated that bones are developed first and then it is covered with mscles. Before 42 days embryo cannot be distinguished from embryo of other animals, but at this stage it becomes clearly distinguishable.

"When 42 nights have passed from the time of Nutfah (time of conception), God sends an angel to it, who shapes it and makes its hearing, sight, skin, muscles and bones.....(Narrated by Huzaifa, Sahih Muslim, Kitab Al-Qadar).

Laham(muscles)

We have already seen that skeleton is formed in seventh week and the differenciation of muscles starts in the eighth week, in other words myogenesis takes place during this stage. Development of definitive muscles starts in the trunk and the foetus starts moving, and muscles take their position around the bones. The sequence of events is very fast as is mentioned in the Quran.(use of fa...an Arabic conjunction which means rapid sequence of events). This facg is stated as:

"Then (fa) We clothed the bones with lahm, muscle, flesh)...." (Quran). states the fact as The passage also indicates that lahm stage represents the end of embryonic (takhlik) stage, which is followed by Nashah stage. The conjunction thumma (then) indicates a slow sequence with a time lag between the two stages.

The next stage is **Nashaa (Growth)**

The word Nasha'a in Arabic means: to initiate, grow and develop, to rise and increase. Nashaa phase begins from ninth week to term and is further divided in two stages:

First stage of Nashaa is 'An-Nashaa al khalqan' (Attaining the definite human form) from 9 weeks until 26 weeks. Up to 12 wks the growth is slow but after 12 weeks the overall size of the foetus increases rapidly. Lanugo hair appears on the body. The sex differentiation is possible . By the end of this stage the various organs are fully functioning, e.g: kidneys are forming urine, blood cells are formed in bone marrow and hair follicles appear.

The second stage of Nashaa is Al-Hadanah ar –rahamiya (uterine incubation) begins from 26 weeks to full term (40 weeks by dates). Baby can survive outside without placental or uterine support after 24 to 26 weeks. So, last 3 months can be considered a time for the uterus to provide additional support and a place for normal growth.

The term "nash'ah" clearly and accurately describes this stage of intra uterine development. The meaning to "initiate, describes the initial functioning of various organs and systems. The second meaning "to grow" indicates the rapid growth and the development of various organs. The third meaning "to rise and increase" describes the very rapid and obvious increase in foetal size and weight.

"He makes you in the wombs of your mothers in stages, one after another, in three veils of darkness.." (Quran: Surah Az-zumar, (39:6)) Quran accurately described the three veils of Darkness, Anterior abdominal wall, the uterine wall and Amnio-chorionic membrane that surrounds the embryo.

In the second century AD, Galen had described the placenta and membranes in his book 'on the Formation of a Foetus'. In the 15-th century Leonardo da Vinci drew an illustration of "foetus in a womb". We cannot be certain when scholars realized that human beings developed in uterus surrounded by three membranes.

Until late 19th century, Scholars held the Aristotle's view that foetus was formed from menstrual blood and other imaginative theories without any scientific proof. Many Muslim scholars refuted those views on the basis of this Quranic verses like:

"Was he not a drop of germinal fluid emited"? (Quran, Al-Qiyamah(75:37)).

In 1448 AD, for example, Ibn-Hajer wrote in 'Fath-Al-Bari (Vol 2; p 447–491)': "....Many Anatomists claim that the male fluid has no effect on the creation of child except for coagulation of blood and that the child is formed from the menstrual blood. However, prophet's Hadeeth in this chapter refutes this claim"

Only since 19th century, scientists started to understand the precise steps and stages in the development of human embryo. Dr. Keith Moore (one of the highest authorities in the field of embryology) surveyed the Quranic verses and realized that Muslims had this knowledge since seventh century. He said, until 30 years back, scientists lacked such knowledge. Dr. Keith Moore further said: "It is clear to me that these statements (in Quran, about embryologic development) must have come to Muhammad from God, because almost all of this knowledge was not discovered until many centuries later. This proves to me that Muhammad must have been a Messenger of God."

"Soon we will show them our signs in the (furthest) regions (of the earth), and in their own selves, until it becomes manifest to them that this is the truth. Is it not enough that your Lord does witness all things".
(Quran, Fussilat, (41:53))

---

8 OPENING OF SEVENTH SEAL, FOUR ANGELS BLOW TRUMPETS (RV.8)

RV.8: 1-2 When he had opened the seventh seal, there was silence in heaven for about half hour. Then the seven angels who stood before God were given seven trumpets.

[How did they keep time, without sun and moon?]

RV.8: 3-5 Another angel carrying a golden censer came and stood at the altar. Much incense was given to him to offer it with the prayers of all saints on the golden altar that was before the throne. The smoke of the incense, along with the prayers of the saints, ascended up before God. The angel took the censer and filled it with fire of the altar and threw it into the earth and there were voices and thunders and lightnings and an earthquake.

[The angel burned mixture of incense and prayers of saints. And smoke rose up to God. When the incense was used up, he put some burning coal into the censor and dumped the loaded censor on to earth. The impact caused an earthquake. Thunder and lightning and voices arose from the impact site. At time of Moses, priests used to dump ashes and residue from burning carcasses on the ground near the altar. In heaven the altar is set up in front of the throne on stage and no trash can was set up near the altar. So, at the end of the incense burning ceremony, the angles dump the ashes and residue on earth. That explains frequent earth quakes and thunders and lightnings on earth!]

RV.8: 6-11 The seven angels which had the seven trumpets prepared themselves to blow. The first angel blew and hail and fire mingled with blood fell on earth and all green grass and a third of all trees were burnt up. The second angel blew and a great ball of fire, as big as a mountain, was thrown into the sea and a third of the sea became blood and a third of all life forms in the sea died and a third of the ships were destroyed.The third angel blew, and a great star called 'Wormwood' burning like a lamp, fell from heaven, on third of the rivers and on the water springs. One third of the waters became bitter like wormwood and many men died of the waters.

[John is describing a volcanic eruption on 'Thera' island near Patmos. To make the event supernatural, John burned a third of the trees and made a third of the seas blood and killed a third of the fish and destroyed a third of the ships and poisoned a third of the waters. God and the author did not know that stars are huge in size and they are far away from earth. If a star falls on earth or earth go near star, one third of the waters won't get poisoned, the entire earth will evaporate.

There is only one stream in Patmos. It is possible that one day a tree fell near it and the branches made rot in nthe water and John became sick from drinking that water. So, the mescaline hazed mind of John imagined a star with name wormwood, fell into the water and one third of the water (down stream) became bitter like wormwood. If a star named 'wine' fell into the water, one third of the water would have become wine and many people would have become drunk.

Only God and President Bush can do such precision damage like turning one third of the seas into blood. President Bush used burn the entire cities during Iraq war and call it precision bombing and surgical strikes to take out the terrorists.

Many preachers have suggested that the Chernobyl nuclear disaster was the star mentioned in Revelation. The word Chernobyl, which in Ukrainian language (чорнобиль) means 'wormwood' or 'mugwort'. Chernobyl nuclear meltdown did release radiation and contaminated the lakes and rivers and land and air near it. Many men and animals died. As far as we know, there are no stars with name Chernobyl.]

RV.8: 12 The fourth angel sounded and one third of the sun and the moon and the stars were darkened. On a third part of the earth, light did not shine during day and also during night.

[In the modern world of science, such descriptions may seem silly and ignorant. However it made a lot of sense to the people for whom these revelations were intended. Modern day theologians try to explain it all as figurative. But John wrote it as literal. Why insult the author by telling that it was all figurative. After saying it is all figurative, they try to explain the literal meaning of it anyway and they fail.

According to Prophet Mohammed, at the end of the world, one shout (compare to one blow of trumpet) will make all living things, including angels and heavenly creatures, die. God will roll up the earth and the whole universe in his hands (like a scroll). Sun and moon will be darkened. Stars will fall. Mountains will be crushed into fine powder. On the second shout, every creature that ever lived on earth will be re-created. Then, there will be the judgment process.

Why do Christian God and Angels use trumpets while Muslim God use shouts? Christians (Jews who believed in Jesus) were used to reading about Moses using trumpets for commanding his army in OT. Also, the followers of Jesus were ruled by Romans. At the time of Jesus, Romans were using trumpet for issuing military commands to soldiers and in battlefields. Jews learned from their masters. So, in Christian mythology, Gods send out angels to blow trumpets to issue commands. Arabs in seventh century were shouting out commands in battlefields. Thus in Muslim heaven, God shouts instead of asking angels to blow trumpets.]

RV.8: 13 I saw an angel flying through the middle of heaven, announcing in loud voice: 'Misery, misery, misery, to those who live on earth at blowing of the trumpets of the three angels, who are yet to blow!

[In public boxing matches, a scantily clad young woman would walk around on the stage holding up a sign saying 'Round 3', for example. This is to notify the audience that the next is, 'third round'. Same situation in haven also. An angel is flying around announcing the coming attractions. Residents of heaven should look down to earth if they want to watch the next sadistic event on earth.]

9 FIFTH ANGEL BLOWS, PLAGUE OF LOCUSTS FROM HELL, SIXTH ANGEL BLOWS, HORSEMEN FROM EUPHRATES (RV. 9)

RV.9: 1-2 Then the fifth angel blew and a star fell from heaven to the earth and the key of the bottomless pit was given to him. He opened the bottomless pit. Out of the pit, smoke arose as from a large furnace and the smoke darkened the sun and the air.

[First sun and moon were darkened and stars fell. Then one third of sun and moon were darkened and one third of stars fell to earth. Now, a star fell to earth from heaven. Is this a star like sun or is this a rock-and-roll star like Michael Jackson? Morning star is portrayed as a person, for exmple. Anyway, the star is a man and he was given the key to bottomless pit.

Now what is a bottomless pit? Is it a black hole in space? It could be an elastic pit which expands as much as needed so that it will never reach a bottom limit. Some preachers have suggested that the bottomless pit is in the center of earth because anything that falls into it will never hit a bottom because gravity pulls everything to the center of earth. But if everything is suspended in the center, then that will be considered the bottom, won't it? Psychoanalysts say the idea of a bottomless pit was developed in the minds of men after experiencing the seemingly endlessly stretchy nature of the vaginal canal.

Smoke from the bottomless pit has darkened the sun and moon and the air. People on earth are groping in the dark. Can John still look down from heaven and see the locusts and stuff on earth in this darkness?]

RV.9: 3-4 Locusts came out of the smoke upon the earth and they were given power, as the scorpions of the earth have power. They were commanded not to hurt the grass of the earth or green thing or tree; but only those men which have not the seal of God in their foreheads.

[All the grass and one third of the trees were burned up already. So, the locusts could not hurt the grass. These locusts were special purpose locusts from hell with face recognition technology. They will attack men who do not have the seal of God on their foreheads. Until recently, descriptions like this were scoffed off as fantasy. But, modern technology allows robots to do just these kinds of things. Parking meters read license plates of cars in parking spaces. Cameras identify person in a crowd by face recognition and by gait and by voice and by biometric recognition. Specific people in a crowd can be attacked and disabled or crippled or even killed by robots or drones.]

RV.9: 5-11 They were not to kill but only to inflict pain like from scorpion-venom for five months. In those days, men shall seek death and shall not find it; and shall desire to die, and death shall flee from them. The shapes of the locusts were like horses prepared for battle. It appeared as if they had golden crowns on their heads. Their faces were like faces of men. They had hair like hair of women and they had teeth similar to the teeth of lions. They had breastplates, as if it were breastplates of iron; and the sound of their wings was as the sound of chariots of many horses running to battle. They had tails like that of scorpions and there were stings in their tails. They were given power to hurt men for five months. They had a king over them, who is the angel of the bottomless pit, whose name is Abaddon in Hebrew and Apollyon in Greek.

[Here John is describing a modern robots or drones or helicopters. John was not familiar with any modern machinery or weaponry. If he saw or heard anything moving or flying, he would describe it as a creature. A rocket or missile with 'US ARMY' written on it, fired from a silo will be described as a beast with blasphemy written on its forehead coming out of his bottomless pit and smoke rose and blocked sun and moon and there was a big earthquake and thunders and lightnings and voices and one third of the island was destroyed.

Prophet Mohammed also made many pronouncements which nobody understood until 1400 years later in the light of modern science. For example, (Quran, 24:40) says: ***"Or (the unbelievers' state) is like the***

darkness in a deep sea. It is covered by waves, above which are waves, above which are clouds. Darknesses, one above another. If a man stretches out his hand, he cannot see it.... "

This verse mentions the darkness found in deep seas and oceans, where if a man stretches out his hand, he cannot see it. Around a depth of 200 meters and below, there is pitch darkness in the oceans. Below a depth of 1000 meters there is absolute darkness. In those days, there were no scuba diving equipment, and human beings could only dive a few meters. Even with scuba diving equipment human beings cannot dive more than 30 meters. Below that submarines are needed. 1400 years ago, no human being could have known about the darkness in the depth of seas.

The above Quranic verse also says there are waves and then waves above them and above them skies. 1400 years after Quran was revealed, in the 20th century, scientists have discovered the 'internal waves'. It is not visible to human eyes. In the depth of oceans there are waves called internal waves, just like surface waves. Between 1974 and 1994, oceanographer Dr. Jacques Cousteau, with modern equipment and measurements, found out that it was true. There are waves below the surface just like the waves above. Prophet Mohammed was illiterate and he has never seen sea in his life time. Dr. Jacques Cousteau concluded that only God could have told Mohammed, these oceanographic scientific truths. Dr. Jacques Cousteau secretly converted to Islam, to the dismay of his family and countrymen. After his death, his family tried to protect his reputation in France, which is a predominantly Catholic country, by denying that he converted to Muslim religion.]

RV.9: 12-16 One misery is past. Look, there come two more miseries. The sixth angel blew his trumpet and a voice from the four horns of the golden altar which is before God, was heard: 'Loose the four angels which are bound in the great river Euphrates.' The four angels were loosed. Each of them were prepared to slay a third of men for an hour, for a day, for a month, and for a year. I heard the horsemen numbered 2 million.

[This is a huge army, even by today's standard. At the time of John, two million horsemen was unbelievably large number. The largest number they could write in Roman numerals was a million. John wrote two times thousand times thousand. This is more than the world population of the time. (World comprised of Palestine area and some Goym (Samaritans) and some Greeks and Romans.) In modern days, it would be equivalent to saying the army was 1 billion strong and each was driving a tank.

Compare this to the famous and decisive battle of 'Badr' where the forces of Prophet Mohammed decisively defeated Meccan army. The Meccan army consisted of almost a thousand Meccans with 100 horses and 170 camels. Prophet Mohammed had about 300 men, 2 horses and 70 camels. In the battle all Meccan leaders died. Muslims buried the dead enemies. Muslims took a large number of prisoners.

The prisoners were treated better than the captors. Prisoners rode the horses and camels while their captors walked through the desert. The prisoners were given the best food they had while their captors chewed on pits of dates imagining it was dates and drank water and went hungry. So, the victorious army walked back to their home city hungry and exhausted with their well-fed and rested prisoners riding on horses and camels. Those prisoners who were poor were freed immediately. Those prisoners who could read and write were freed in return for teaching 10 Muslims each how to read and write. Mohammed could not read or write. Those few prisoners who could afford to pay a Ransom were freed when their family paid a ransom. When the families refused to pay, they were allowed to go free anyway. The prisoners were so amazed at the generosity of their captors, they decided not to go home when they were freed; instead most of them stayed with Muslims. Nobody was water boarded or tortured in secret CIA prisons and nobody was held without trial and tortured and raped in Abu Graib or Guantanamo. Muslim religion prohibits mistreatment of prisoners of war.]

RV.9: 17 The horses I saw in the vision had heads like that of lions and fire and smoke and sulfur issued out of their mouths. Those who sat on them had breastplates made of fire, reddish brown zircon and sulfur.

[John has never seen any modern weaponry. The combat helicopters will be flying grasshoppers with the sound of thousand horsemen riding to battle. Artillery and RPG and shoulder fired missiles would be grotesque creatures that talk like thunder and spit out sulfur and fire and smoke. The exhaust coming out of a tank or APV would look like fire and smoke coming out of the mouths or tails of the dragons.]

RV.9: 18-19 One third of all men were killed by the fire and smoke and sulfur which issued from their mouths. Their power is in their mouth and in their tails because their tails were like that of serpents and had heads and they hurt with them.

[John is describing modern tanks or other mechanism on the battle field. It was precision bombing or surgical strike as American military would say, that is why precisely one third of men were killed.]

RV.9: 20-21 The men who survived these plagues did not repent their evil deeds. Nor did they repent their worship of devils and idols of gold and silver and brass and stone and wood, which neither can see, nor hear, nor walk. Nor did they repent of their murders and sorceries and fornication and thefts.

[May be those people did not know about God at that time. In modern times, Christian churches have become museums and faith in God has been replaced by science and technology. Calamities will not force people to worship god. Instead, people will think of new technologies to overcome those disasters. Prophet Mohammed said that in the last days, Quran and memory of God will be removed from this world. People will say: 'We have heard from our grandparents that people used to say 'There is no God besides God' but we don't know what that means.']

.

.

.

.

10 WORDS OF SEVEN THUNDERS, JOHN EATS SWEET AND BITTER LITTLE BOOK (RV.10)

RV.10: 1-4 Another mighty angel came down from heaven, wearing a cloud. He had a rainbow on his head. His face shone like the sun and his feet were like pillars of fire. He had a little book open in his hand and he set his right foot on the sea and his left foot on the earth and cried out in a loud voice, like a lion's roar. Then seven thunders spoke. And I was about to write when a voice from heaven told me: 'Seal up those things which the seven thunders spoke, and do not write them'.

[Until now, we thought perhaps Jesus raised John to heaven and put on a show for him and he wrote about things he saw with his eyes and heard with his ears. Now, we are told that John did not ascend to heaven. He was sitting in his room and writing and everything he saw was his own imagination in his head.

Well, it could be visions. Vision is seeing something like an apparition. For example the three children in Fatima apparently saw mother Mary while they were shepherding. If they saw something in the skies, then that would be a vision. It is real to them, even if the other people who assembled there did not see anything.

Many of the things John described could not have been seen even in a vision. It had to be just wild fantasy, aided by mescaline or equivalent. But can it be pure fantasy when many of the things John described are also found in other books of Bible and also in Quran? John repeats or expands many of the ideas given in Gospels and Old Testament. That is why his words match with what is in OT, NT and even Quran. For example the statement 'sun and moon darkened' is in Gospels and in OT and in Quran.]

RV.10: 5-7 The angel who stood on the sea and on the earth raised his hand to heaven and swore by the immortal who created heaven and earth and the sea and everything in it, that there should be time no longer: but in the days of the voice of the seventh angel, when he shall begin to sound, the mystery of God should be finished, as he has declared to his servants the prophets.

[If the immortal who is sitting on the throne is the creator of the universe, then he must be God the father. Until now, we were given the impression that it was somebody who shall not die again (immortal), or Jesus himself. Now, we are told that he is God the father.

It is interesting to note that God created heaven and earth and Sea. The primordial sea is separate from both heaven and earth.]

RV.10: 8 The heavenly voice spoke to me again and said: 'Go and take the little book which is open in the hand of the angel who stands on the sea and on the earth'.

[If John had to take the little book from the hand of the angel, the book had to be of small size and angel had to be of John's size. If the angel was of John's size he must have been standing on the shore of the sea with one foot in water. The sea must have been still. If there were waves, both feet would be periodically in the sea.]

RV.10: 9-11 I went and asked the angel: 'Give me the little book'. He told me: 'Take it, and eat it up; and it shall make your belly bitter; but it shall be in your mouth sweet as honey'. I took the little book out of the angel's hand and ate it up; and it was sweet as honey in my mouth. As soon as I had eaten it, my belly was bitter. He told me: 'you must prophesy again before many peoples and nations and languages and kings'.

[So, John ate up the little edible book. In the sixties and seventies sex shops used to sell edible panties that was made with colored pasta for women. Men could undress the women by eating up their panties. This was supposed to be very erotic. Here John ate a thin, small, scroll-shaped cake laced with mescaline and honey. In those days books were written in scrolls. The sugar in it gave him acid stomach and the mescaline in it made him feel like he is a prophet. The angel told him to go and prophecy to people of many tribes and languages and kings. During the sixties, 'Hippies' used to carry around and eat blotting paper that was previously dipped in acid (LSD). The word Hippie came from the attitude of the young people that it was 'Hip' or 'Uppity' or 'fashionable' to be carefree, acid smoking, free-loving, dropouts. Here, John is ingesting his dope mixed with tubular pieces of cake or bread.]

.

.

.

.

.

.

.

.

.

.

.

.

.

.

.

.

.

11 MEASUREMENT OF TEMPLE, THREE WOES TO MEN, TEMPLE OF GOD IN HEAVEN OPENED (RV.11)

RV.11: 1-4 I was given a reed-like measuring stick and the angel said: 'Rise, and measure the temple of God and the altar and those who worship in it.

Don't measure the court yard outside the temple because it is given to the Gentiles. For forty two months they shall tread the holy city under their feet. I will give power to my two witnesses and they shall prophesy twenty four thousand and sixty days, wearing sackcloth. They are the two olive trees and the two candlesticks standing before the God of the earth.'

[John tells that the stage on which the end-of-time show was put on was in the temple of God in heaven. In the temple, there is a throne. On the throne there are four beasts covered with eyes all over and inside. These beasts are constantly praising the immortal man sitting on the throne, like a cassette player in a loop. (Cassette player is an instrument which was very popular in 1960's and 1970's. Then DVDs became popular in the 1980's and then solid state memory in the 2000's.)

The immortal is presumed God, because thunder and lightning and voices shoots out of the throne constantly, which according to OT is the sign of presence of God. He is referred to as the immortal man. In front of the throne there are seven candle sticks which are seven angels of the seven Christian congregations in Asia. The throne is surrounded by 24 Elders of unknown origin, with crowns. They all have pocket harps which they pull out and play any time to praise the immortal man on the throne. In front of the throne is a Crystal glass Sea. In front of the throne there is also an altar with fire burning all the time. Tens of thousands of souls of victims of Jewish persecution of Christians hide under the altar. When the sixth trumpet was blown, they rose up from under the altar and asked the immortal man, to take revenge on their slayers still living on earth. The immortal man gave them white gowns and promised to take revenge after the rest of the souls who are expected to be victims of

Jewish persecution of Christians, has reached heaven after their martyrdom. Countless souls of Goym believers with white gowns and Palm leaves in hands stand in front of the altar. There are innumerable angels behind the throne. They provide the chorus while others sing praises to the immortal man. The seven angels have been given trumpets. They started blowing trumpets one by one bringing in calamities upon the people of earth below.

John is standing next to the twenty-four Elders and watching the show. One angel came and stood on the crystal sea and on the earth. The stage is dirt floor. Cement is not available in heaven. Then, John picked up a small book from the hands of this angel and ate it. It was sweet and after eating it, his stomach became acidic. Acid stomach and vomiting are typical reactions after ingesting mescaline. Then he was told to prophecy. Before he could do that he was asked to measure with a reed, the temple and the people worshipping inside it. Two olive trees and two angels, who were standing in front of the altar, were to be his two witnesses. (Two olive trees and two candlesticks make only two witnesses by heavenly arithmetic.) If anybody tries to hurt the olive trees they will be killed with fire coming out of their mouths. After killing them with fire, their bodies will be left to rot in the street, in the heavenly city called Sodom and Egypt, for three and a half days.

John forgot that there is no death and rotting corpse in heaven. It is obvious that after eating pieces of mescaline pie John has been confused. What is the meaning of all this? Obviously nothing. For 2000 years learned men have been trying in vain, to make sense out of all these ramblings.]

RV.11: 5 And if any man shall hurt them, fire proceeds out of their mouth, and devours and kills their enemies:

[Here, John may be describing a modern flame thrower. But how can a flame thrower kill a heavenly creature? Men go to heaven after being dead and then resurrected. Life in heaven is eternal. Mortals do not live in heaven. Flame throwing won't kill anybody in heaven.]

RV.11: 6 These have power to shut heaven, so that it does not rain in the days of their prophecy: and have power over waters to turn them to blood, and to hit the earth with all plagues, as often as they will.

[These heavenly creatures have great powers: they can stop the rain while they are prophesying. They can turn water into blood and hit the earth with plagues. Why do they have to stop rain while prophesying? Because when somebody is prophesying, people gather around to hear it. If there is a rain, the people will run away and seek shelter. So, they have to make sure the rain is stopped. But people will run away if there is a big tornado or earth quake or an attack by a band of rabid dogs also.

What exactly is the prophecy good for? So far nothing useful came out of the book of Revelation. Prophecy means something that is going to happen. If something is going to happen that is going to happen. What good does it do to hear about it? If the prophecy is that Mr. A is going to die of a heart attack at 10 am, what good would it do for him to hear about it? May be he will be careful or stay in a hospital. If he survives the 10 am heart attack, that means he did not die as prophesied. So it was a false prophecy. If he dies, then it means that knowing about it in advance did not do any good, anyway. So, hearing about the so-called prophecy is useless.

Prophecies are usually un-decipherable riddles. Jesus prophesied that the world was going to end in the lifetime of his peers. It did not happen. Jesus prophesied that he will be alive in the belly of the earth for three days and three nights like Jonas was alive in the belly of the fish for three days and three nights. Jesus was alive in the tomb, but only for one day and two nights. The Jewish priests and Pharisees were waiting for him to come out on the third day so that they can capture him and kill him again. So, if any prophecy ever came true, at least partially, it was that of Jesus about his own death and burial and resurrection.

In the current situation, John is talking about the two witnesses, the trees, and candle sticks, prophesying. They are already in heaven. Are they prophesying to the angels, about what will happen to them? Do angels care about any of this stuff?

They can turn water into blood and afflict earth with pestilence. Who cares? These are end-times. The world has already ended. The sun and moon were darkened and the stars fell, and the universe was rolled up like a scroll. It is all over. At this point who cares about the color of water or rain or pestilence? Do dead people care about these things? So, this is all just scare talk to intimidate illiterate Asian villagers.]

RV.11: 7 After they finish their testimony, the beast that ascends out of the bottomless pit shall fight with them and shall overcome them, and kill them.

[The devil rose from bottomless pit and went to heaven and killed the two olive trees and two candlesticks that were standing in front of God.]

RV.11: 8 And their dead bodies shall lie in the street of the great city, which spiritually is called Sodom and Egypt, where also our Master was crucified.

[Jerusalem is called Sodom and also Egypt. It is appropriate names for the modern city of Jerusalem. In 2014, Jerusalem was declared the homosexual capital of the world and the most LGBT friendly city of the world. It is also the world capital of the child pornography and adult and gay pornography and prostitution and sex slave trafficking.]

RV.11: 9 The families and people of different languages and tribes shall see their dead bodies three and half days and shall not allow their dead bodies to be buried.

[Dead bodies lying there unburied and rotting in the streets of heaven? can heavenly creatures die?]

RV.11: 10-13 Those who live on earth shall rejoice over them, and make merry, and shall send gifts one to another because these two prophets tormented those who lived on earth. After three and half days, the Spirit of life from God entered into them, and they stood upon their feet; and those who saw them were greatly afraid. They heard a loud voice from heaven: 'Come up here'. And they ascended up to heaven in a cloud and their enemies saw them. In the same hour, there was a big earthquake, and the tenth part of the city fell, and seven thousand men were killed and the remaining people were frightened and praised God of heaven.

[Nobody knows to this day what John is talking about here. He is telling about two people (the two olive trees and two candlesticks) who preached gospel (?) and they were killed by people and they were brought back to life by God and then taken to heaven. God punished the city for killing them with an earth quake and destruction of one tenth of the city and death of 7000 people. (So, the total population was 10 x 7000 = 70,000).]

RV.11: 14-15 The second misery is past. Look, the third misery comes quickly. The seventh angel blew and there were loud voices in heaven: 'The kingdoms of this world have become the kingdoms of our God and of his 'anointed one', and he shall reign for ever and ever'.

[The God who created the infinitely vast universe and everything in it and the God who controls everything down to the greying of a hair on a man's head, finally got control of the kingdoms of the world! The heavenly creatures were very happy and they loudly announced God's victory!! Now they can travel to any of these kingdoms without a visa. Now, these kingdoms will have to pay tribute to God. Wow, what a victory! This proves once and for all that if God tries hard and persist he can defeat even some men of earth!]

RV.11: 16-18 The twenty four elders, who sat before God on their seats, fell upon their faces, and worshipped God, saying: 'We give you thanks, O Master, almighty God, who is and was and is to come; because you have taken your great power and have reigned. The tribes were angry and your wrath has come and the time of the dead to be judged and the time to destroy those who destroy the earth and the time to give reward to your servants: the prophets and the saints and those who fear your name from all walks of life.'

RV.11: 19 The temple of God was opened in heaven. In his temple a wooden box containing his Law was seen. There were lightning and thunder and voices and an earthquake and great hail.

[In TV shows of 70's and 80's with live audience, a sign in front of the audience will flash 'laughter', 'clap' 'standing ovation' etc. and the studio audience will follow instructions. Just like those live audience, the 24 Elders of unknown origin (they could be humanoid robots), on cue, fall on their faces and worship the eternal man on the throne!

The lightning and loud voices, and thunder and earthquake and great hail are coming from the wooden box. Because God sits on top of the wooden box, just as written in the book of Exodus, guarding the Law (10 commandments) and Moses's diary. Wherever god is, there would be thunder and lightning and earthquake and voices. Remember, the earth quake and lightning and hail etc. are happening in heaven. The earth has already been rolled up like a scroll by God in previous chapter. If the earth quake (shake), will it be felt in the heavens?]

.

.

.

.

.

.

.

.

.

.

.

12 WOMAN WITH A CHILD, DRAGON MAKE WAR WITH ANGELS AND PROGECNY OF WOMAN (RV.12)

RV.12: 1 A great wonder appeared in heaven: a woman wearing sun as her cloth, and standing on the moon and wearing a crown of twelve stars on her head.

[John is describing the picture of Goddess Diana he saw in the great 'Temple of Diana' in Patmos Island.]

RV.12: 2-4 She is pregnant and delivering a child and she cried in pain. Another wonder appeared in heaven: a great red dragon, having seven heads and ten horns, and seven crowns upon his heads. His tail drew one third of the stars of heaven and threw them to the earth. The dragon stood before the woman who was delivering, to devour her child as soon as it was born.

[Now, try to top that for a revelation or prophecy of future! At the time of John, dragons (dinosaurs) still roamed the earth. (The evolutionists tell us these dragons disappeared from the earth 65 million years ago and then humans came into existence. They say this with a straight face even though dinosaur bones with blood and bone marrow were found and live dinosaurs were sighted in 20th century. The evolutionists and the holocaust propagandists both believe that they can perpetuate a lie by constantly repeating it in mass media.) John probably saw a dragon in Patmos Island. John wrote about a dragon with 10 heads in the sea. So, this dragon pulled down with his tail one third of the stars in heaven and threw it onto earth. Then he came and stood before the woman in between her legs to eat the child as soon as he is born. The dragon which pulled down stars is very big. If he has to stand between her legs to catch the child as soon as it comes out, she must have very long legs. What is the size of this woman? John already told us that she was a heavenly wonder. She wore sun as her cloth, moon at het feet and 12 stars on her head. This woman is as big as the milkyway galaxy!]

RV.12: 5-6 She delivered a boy who was to rule all tribes with a rod of iron. The boy caught up to God and his throne. The woman fled into the wilderness, where god has prepared a place for her and there they shall feed her for 24060 days.

[So, the dragon was standing in between the legs of the woman with his mouth open in front of her opening to catch the baby as soon as it comes out. Then the baby came out. It immediately jumped on to God and his throne and escaped the dragon. It was a gymnastic baby. Why didn't the dragon eat the woman while the baby was still inside her? We will never know. May be Dragons are stupid. But this is not just any dragon; it is the Satan, the Devil, the deceiver of the whole world. May be it is all a divine mystery.

Naturally the dragon will go after the woman next. But the woman ran away to her mountain hideout which God had prepared in advance for her. There, God has stored enough canned food and water to feed her for 24060 days (65 + years). God is very smart. He thinks like a modern survivalist. He knows what is needed to survive an angry dragon Satan. The Christian apologists may invent deep meanings for the number 24060. But, there is no deep meaning to this number. It is just a convenient large number which rhymes in Greek.]

RV.12: 7-9 In heaven, Michael and his angels fought against the dragon and his angels. The dragon and his angels lost and they lost their place in heaven. The great dragon, that old serpent called the Devil and Satan, which deceives the whole world, was thrown out into the earth along with his angels.

[The Christian apologists, especially those on the payroll of Zionists and Mossad keep interpreting the woman as Mary and the child as Jesus. According to this book of Revelation, Jesus was born and he ascended to the throne of God and then Michael and his angels fought with Satan and his angels. Satan and his angels were thrown out of heaven and into the earth. So, the devil came to earth only after Jesus came and went. If that is true, there should have been no evil on earth until two thousand years ago. Didn't devil deceive Eve in Garden east of Eden? Didn't Devil test Jesus in the desert? Didn't Devil enter the heart of Judas? But the preachers on Zionist payroll don't use logic when discussing Revelation. They just want to use the Revelation to prove that Christians should support the modern country of Israel in every evil thing they do, including killing Christians and Muslims of Palestine and taking their land and property and their organs (body parts).]

RV.12: 10-12 I heard a loud voice in heaven: 'Now salvation and strength and the kingdom of our God and the power of his 'anointed one' has come; because the accuser of our brethren, who accused them before our God day and night, is thrown down. They overcame him by the blood of the Lamb and by their statement. They did not love their life more than death. Therefore rejoice heavens and those who live in heaven. Misery to the inhabitants of the earth and the sea! Because the devil has come down to you, with great anger, because he knows that he has only a short time.'

[For 2000 years pundits have tried to make sense out of these statements in vain. Who is the accuser of the brethren? Satan? He accused them of what? Accused them in front of God, day and night? Then they (who are these they? Michael and his angels?) Overcame Satan by the blood of the lamb? Is that lamb Jesus? So, this struggle happened after Jesus was crucified? How did Michael overcome Satan with blood of Lamb? Did he throw some of the blood into Satan's eyes and blinded him? The only possible explanation is this: John was high on mescaline.

Did the loud voice in heaven come from the heavenly PA system? Previously we were told that angels fly through the middle of heavens and make live public announcements.]

RV.12: 13-14 When the dragon realized that he was thrown out into earth, he persecuted the woman who delivered the boy. Two wings of a large eagle were given to the woman so that she might fly into the wilderness, into her place, where she is nourished for two and one half periods of time, from the face of the serpent.

RV.12: 15-17 Serpent spit out a flood after the woman, so that the flood might carry her away. The earth helped the woman, and the earth opened her mouth, and swallowed up the flood. The dragon was angry with the woman, and went to make war with the remnant of her seed, which keep the commandments of God and have the testimony of Jesus Christ.

[John is trying to copy some of the Greek mythology here. A dragon dragged one third of all stars and dropped them into earth! The dragon was devil. He was thrown out of heaven on to earth. Earth seems to be the dumping ground for all the heavenly garbage.

Then the Satan tried to swallow her son as soon as he was born. But he jumped and caught up with God and his throne. The woman was given two wings of a large eagle and she flew to a forest hideout. Then the dragon spit out a flood to wash away the woman. But Earth, which is also a live creature, opened its mouth and swallowed all that flood. Now, we all know what is the source of all this water on earth. Then the dragon went to war with the remnant if her progeny which keeps the commandments of God and teachings of Jesus. Wait a minute, where did all this remnant of her progeny come from? Did she deliver many children before the son who escaped dragon? Also, all this happened after the death of Jesus. Because the remnant of her progeny kept the teachings of Jesus. So, this war took place barely two thousand years ago on this earth. So, it should be in some history books.]

.

.

.

.

.

.

.

13 THE BEAST NAMED BLASPHEMY WITH SEVEN HEADS AND TEN HORNS (RV.13)

RV.13: 1 I stood on the sandy beach and saw a beast with seven heads and ten horns, and ten crowns on horns, and the name 'blasphemy' written on forehead, rise out of the sea.

[Here is the mother of all 'Loch Ness Monsters'. John, standing on the Psili Ammos beach, the only sandy beach on Patmos Island, probably saw a lava flow from the volcano eruption on the nearby island of Thera. When the lava flows into the sea, it snakes into the sea through multiple channels and when the hot lava hit the water, it explodes and steam rises up like a beast hissing, and solidifies and become like a dragon or beast with multiple heads.]

RV.13: 2 The beast which I saw was like a leopard, with feet of a bear and mouth of a lion. The dragon gave the beast his power and his seat and great authority.

[Has John ever seen a leopard or bear or lion? Probably, not. He is just throwing out all the fierce animals he has heard about, to give the beast a fierce look. For one thing the beast was standing in the water. Did John go up close and look under water to see what his feet look like? The feet of a leopard are not much different from the feet of a bear in the eye of a human being watching from a distance. What is the difference between the mouth of a lion and the mouth of a leopard? Both animals are from the same 'cat' family. John did not see anything. He just made up an imaginary super beast by combining different animals he has heard about. He was following the example of the statue made of gold, silver, bronze, iron and clay, described in Daniel 2. Or perhaps John saw a genetic mutation. Nah, he just made it up.

Daniel 2 tells an incredible story. The author of Daniel's story made it up also. It was a version of the story of Joseph. Joseph saw a dream and interpreted it and Pharaoh put him in charge of Egypt. Joseph's story could have been based on a true story. Because Quran also talks about Joseph and his getting honors for interpreting a dream. Just like Joseph, Daniel interprets a dream which nobody else could interpret. Joseph's interpretation could be verified in the near future. Nebuchadnezzar's dream would never be verified by Nebuchadnezzar or his successors and it had no practical value. And the predictions did not come true, to boot. Daniel said after four kings, all of them would be destroyed and replaced by an everlasting kingdom. Where is that everlasting kingdom? Perhaps the coming New World Order organized by Zionists will be that perpetual kingdom. Preachers have been trying to make Daniel's interpretation fit with historical facts for millennia without success. Daniel's multi-metal statue is John's mixed animal beast.

How did John know about who gave the beast his power and his authority? What authority? A spectator who is standing far away on the beach will not know these things about a beast which just popped out of the water in the sea; but the author of the fiction would know because he conjures up all these things in his imagination.]

RV.13: 3 One of his heads appeared as if it was wounded to death; and his deadly wound was healed. And all the world wondered after the beast.

[How can John, standing on the beach tell if the beast is dead or alive without getting close and checking pulse or breathing?

One of the channels of the lava-flow had red hot lava at the forward part. As it cooled, the red color of the hot lava was still visible in the middle. So, John thought this was a bloody wound on one of the heads of the beast. Then that red hot part also cooled by the sea and the whole lava head became same color. John describes this as the healing of the wound.

'The world wondered after the beast' is poetic license. The whole world was not standing there on the beach with John and watching this. So, how could John say the whole world wondered about this beast because the deadly blood colored wound healed or the red hot lava that was visible cooled into a solid dark color like the rest of the lava channel. An observer watching this from a distant beach cannot know if the whole world knew about what he saw or how they felt about this incident. But the author of fiction knows all this because he conjures up all these things in his mind.]

RV.13: 4-5 They worshipped the dragon which gave power to the beast: and they worshipped the beast, saying: 'Who is comparable to the beast? Who can fight with him?' He was given a mouth speaking great things and blasphemies; and power was given to him to continue forty two months.

[Who worshipped dragon? Possibly, the human beings who were still on earth. The sun and moon were darkened. The heaven and earth was rolled up like a scroll. One third of all the stars were thrown to earth. Then Jesus was born. Then, Satan was thrown down to earth, etc. . There were still some people left on earth. How did they manage to see the beast that came up in the middle of the sea near the Patmos Island? Most probably, the world population was reduced substantially by all these supernatural calamities, and the only people remaining on earth were on Patmos Island. They were standing on the same beach with John watching everything! That is how John could see and hear what the whole world was thinking, saying and doing.

The whole incident is very cartoonish. The beast was given a mouth to speak great things and blasphemies. Then he was given enough energy to continue for forty two months. After forty two months, the beast would be dead as a toy without battery. The preachers who try hard to find deep meaning to all these baloney are even more cartoonish.]

RV.13: 6-8 He spoke blasphemy against God, his name, his tent and those who lived in heaven. He was allowed to make war with the saints, and to overcome them. He was given power over all families and languages and tribes. All those who live on earth whose names are not written in the book of life of the Lamb slain from the foundation of the world, shall worship him.

[Who gave permission to make war with and win against the saints etc.? There were some folks whose names were not in the book of life. These must be the mud-people who were animals created in the shape of God, on the sixth day of creation. God did not give those animals souls, by blowing into their nostrils. These were soul-less animals in human form. They are referred to as goym (filthy animals) by Jews to this day. Even Jesus refused to heal the daughter of a Goym woman. So, it is those non-Jews who are still left in the world who will worship the Beast. By the way, the Eastern European Jews are Goym. They were nature worshipping nomads of the steppes of Kazakhstan until the 10th century when they converted to Talmudic Judaism.]

RV.13: 9 Let men who have ear hear.

[So, John is asking all those with ears to hear his fantastic story. In his time, there were no fantasy games on handheld computers. So, reading his book was the only alternative.]

RV.13: 10 He who leads into captivity shall go into captivity; he who kills with the sword must be killed with the sword. Here is the patience and the faith of the saints.

[This is not a revelation. This sentence does not belong here. This was probably a later interpolation.]

RV.13: 11-12 I saw another beast coming up out of the earth. He had two horns like a lamb and he spoke like a dragon. He exercises all the power of the first beast before him and makes the earth and those who live in it to worship the first beast, whose deadly wound was healed.

[Patmos Island apparently had a lot of mutant creatures. First beast came out of sea. Second beast came out of the earth. Lambs generally have no horns. May be John saw some lambs with horn in Patmos Island. Anyway, these beasts have horns like lamb. This creature talks like dragon by making hissing sound. Creators of 'Godzilla' and 'Jurassic Park' never acknowledged receiving their inspiration from John's Revelation in Patmos Island.

How did earth worship the dragon? Did earth fall on its face and worship the dragon, like the 24 Elders of heaven?]

RV.13: 13-14 He does great wonders, like making fire come down from heaven on the earth in the sight of men. He deceives those who live on the earth by means of those miracles which he had power to do in the sight of the beast, saying to those who live on the earth that they should make an image to the beast which had the wound by a sword and did live.

[So, the beast was cut by a sword and he lived. It was not a gunshot wound because all the guns were confiscated by the beast long before that.]

RV.13: 15 He had power to give life to the image of the beast, so that the image would speak and kill those who do not worship the image.

[The modern interactive television set meets this criterion. People are already addicted to television sets. It can monitor who is in front of it and what they are doing. Face recognition is already freely used. It can be equipped with killing capability also.]

RV.13: 16-18 He makes all people, both small and big, rich and poor, free and slave, to receive a mark in their right hand or in their foreheads. And no man might buy or sell except those who had the mark or the name of the beast or the number of his name. Here is wisdom. Let those who have understanding count the number of the beast. Because it is the number of a man; and his number is 6,6,6.

[John is talking about a society where only those individuals with a mark of the beast is allowed to buy or sell. It is a digital cash society. In America, paying cash for a hotel room needs to be reported to authorities as a possible criminal activity. Any cash withdrawal or deposit over $3000 needs to be reported to authorities as a possible criminal activity. In many European countries cash is compleely eliminated. Money transactions are possible only with a debit or credit card with an embedded chip in it. The central computer can deny any transaction.

Without approval from central computer, no buying or selling is possible.

Chips are embedded in the body of pets and farm animals for indentification already. Such embedded chips have been tried on children to guard against kidnapping. Tiny chips, less than the thickness of a hair, can be embedded in the body through an injection. Vaccinations are mandatory for everybody already. Chips for identification and for financial transaction are already under trial and soon will be available for general use.

Passports are already embedded with chips for biometric identification. Transportation and buying and selling can be completely controlled by a central computer. Those who do not submit to be digitally chipped can be denied food, shelter, transportation, jobs and medical care.

The number of the beast, the central bankers, who impose these things upon the population, is six, six, six as in six pointed star with six triangles and six sides. That is also true already. All the banks in the world are already owned and operated by people who identify with six pointed star. According to John's Revelation, Jewish bankers like Rothschilds are the Beast, or Devil.]

.

.

.

.

.

.

.

.

.

14 LAMB AND 144000 MEN ON MOUNT ZION, FALL OF BABYLON, GOOD SOULS AND BAD SOULS ARE REAPED FROM EARTH(RV.14)

RV.14: 1 A Lamb along with 144000 men, each with his Father's name written in their foreheads, stood on the mount Zion.

[In Exodus Moses told the people to identify by their father's name (tribe) and be counted. John is using that story to come up with this revelation. John forgot that real God does not need anybody to write any name on their forehead for identification.]

RV.14: 2-3 I heard a voice from heaven, like the sound of waves and of great thunder and of harps. They, along with the four beasts and the elders, sung a new song before the throne. No man could learn that song except the hundred and fourty four thousand redeemed from the earth.

[These 144000 men and the Lamb were standing on mount Zion. Then they sang a song in front of the throne and beasts and 24 elders. So, mount Zion must be in front of the throne. It is not clear if mount Zion come in front of the glass crystal sea or behind it. The real estate in front of the throne is very crowded.]

RV.14: 4-5 These men were not defiled with women because they are virgins. They follow the Lamb wherever he goes. They were redeemed from among men, because they were the firstfruits to God and to the Lamb. There is no guile in their mouths because they are faultless before the throne of God.

[Even though women were created by God, they defile men with all that blood and goo and filth coming out of them regularly. So, virgin men are not defiled and are very clean. They are following the Lamb like chicks follow the mother hen around.

"Jesus saw Nathanael coming to him, and told about him: "Look, an Israelite indeed, in whom is no guile !" (Jn.1:47). Now, John is using that phrase to describe the 144000 men he invented in his Revelation fantasy. How did John get this 144000 exactly? Well, Jacob had 12 sons. Each of the 12 must have had 12 children each, the heavenly math is always perfect. That is 12 x 12 = 144. In heaven everything 1000 times bigger. 144x1000 = 144000. That is 12000 from each of the sons of Jacob whom we call tribes; not one less and not one more. In heaven, everything is too perfect. Now, the question is how did John, an observer standing afar know exactly how many are there in each of the tribal groups? Did he count? Did he Google it? John has no way of knowing all such details. The author of fiction can know all these details precisely because he conjures them up in his imagination.]

RV.14: 6-7 An angel, after preaching the everlasting gospel to people who live on earth, of every tribe and family and language, flew in the middle of heaven, saying in a loud voice: 'Fear God and give praise to him. Because the hour of his judgment has come. Worship the one who made heaven and earth and the sea and the fountains of waters.'

[In John's vision, angels fly around the heaven making public announcements. John never heard about modern PA systems. At the time of John, town criers were employed for making public announcements and royal proclamations. Town crier will stand in the middle of the city square and beat the drum to attract the public's attention and then after people have gathered together around him, he will make the announcements.

The angel is telling the heavenly creatures to worship god who created the heaven, the earth, the sea and the fountains of water. Nobody in heaven, including god, seems to know that sea is a collection of water in a large ditch on earth, and nobody seems to know anything about where the springs of water come from or about the water cycle. Six hundred years after John's revelation, the real Angel Gabriel revealed to Mohammed in understandable words the water cycle. 1400 years after Mohammed, the scientists using modern equipment and weather satellites and weather balloons and airplanes and computers and scientific methodology proved that Mohammed was correct in every minute detail about the rain clouds and formation of hail and thunder and lightning and rain fall and water cycle.]

RV.14: 8 Another angel followed, saying: 'Babylon is fallen, is fallen, that great city, because she made all tribes drink of the wine of the wrath of her fornication'.

[In heaven, the public announcement angels work in tandem, each carrying only a tiny byte of information. Too much information may be too heavy for them to fly around with. An angel loaded with too much public announcements may crash to the floor of heaven and spill all the PA information?

All descendants of Jacob were corrupted by the Babylonian Talmud and Kabbalah written by corrupt, fornicating, filthy Rabbis when they were in Babylon. Jesus came to bring the Jews back from the corruptions of Talmud. John, who was a Greek Jew, blames Babylon for the writing of this filthy book. John says the decline of Babylon was God's punishment for writing Talmud. In the modern world, Jews blame Romans for the crucifixion of Jesus.

The angel repeated the word 'is fallen' twice. Over the last 2000 years, so much has been written and preached about the significance of this repetition. The preachers take every word in Revelation, out of context and parse it and preach up a mountain out of nothing and collect the tithes from the scared believers. The repetition has no relevance except that it rhymes well in Greek.]

RV.14: 9-12 The third angel followed them, saying in loud voice: 'If any man worship the beast and his image, and receive his mark in his forehead, or in his hand, God will be indignant and will torment him with fire and brimstone in the presence of the holy angels and the Lamb and the smoke of their torment will ascend up for ever and he will have no rest day or night. Here is the patience of the saints; here are those who keep the commandments of God and the faith of Jesus.'

[Three angels flew around the heaven in tandem and made three public announcements. The message had no relevance for the inhabitants of heaven. May be these messages were meant only for John who will transmit it to the illiterate Asian Christians.

Receiving mark of the beast was not a voluntary choice. The beast foced it upon the people. People were victims. Now God punish the victims for receiving the mark of the beast. What should people have done: resist the beast and die?]

RV.14: 13 A voice from heaven told me: 'Write: those who die in God are blessed from now on. The spirit says that they may rest from their labors and their works follow them.'

[Dying in God was always considered a blessing. John says it will be a blessing from now on. John is referring to those who die resisiting the beast by not accepting his mark on their foreheads.]

RV.14: 14-16 I saw someone with a golden crown on his head and a sharp sickle in his hand, sitting on a white cloud. Another angel came out of the Temple and cried out to the man who sat on the cloud: 'Thrust in your sickle, and reap. The time is come for you to reap because the harvest of the earth is ripe.' The one who sat on the cloud thrust in his sickle on the earth and the earth was reaped.

[The unknown person with golden crown has not spoken yet. From his appearance, he looks like someone trying to harvest only the good souls. He swung the sickle once and harvested all the chosen ones. This is the rapture which was invented by Nelson Darby in late 19-th century and popularized by that Zionist agent Scofield in the 20-th century.]

RV.14: 17-20 Another angel with a sharp sickle came out of the temple in heaven. An angel who had power over fire came out from the altar and cried out to the angel with sharp sickle: 'Thrust in your sharp sickle and gather the clusters of the vine of the earth; for her grapes are fully ripe.' The angel thrust in his sickle into the earth and gathered the vine of the earth and cast it into the great winepress of the wrath of God. The winepress was trodden outside the city and blood flowed out of the winepress, thousand six hundred furlongs long and up to the horse's bridles deep.

[The bad souls were harvested and taken to the winepress outside the city in heaven. Farmers harvest their grapes and put into winepress and then trample on top of the grapes and squish them and the grape juice will flow out into large vat and then it will be fermented to make wine. The bad souls were harvested and put into these winepresses and angels trampled on them and squished them and their blood flowed into the street. The river of blood was one thousand six hundred furlongs long and up to the bridle-of-the-horses deep, which is about five feet deep. It is easy to figure out how many bad souls were there on earth at time of final harvest. 1600 furlongs long x 10 feet wide by 5 feet deep would be = x gallons of blood. If each person has 1 gallon of blood, then x would be the number of bad souls.]

.

.

.

.

.

.

.

.

.

.

.

15 LAST SEVEN PLAGUES (RV. 15)

RV.15: 1 I saw another great and marvellous miracle in heaven: seven angels filled up with the wrath of God, holding the seven last plagues.

[Angels are like empty bottles. They can be filled with anything. They have been used as candle sticks and witness trees and whatever. Here the angels are filled with wrath (anger) of God. In addition, they are holding the last seven plagues in their hands.]

RV.15: 2-4 Those who had defeated the beast and his image and his mark and the number of his name stand on the sea of glass with the harps of God and it appears like a sea of glass mingled with fire. They sang the song of Moses the servant of God, and the song of the Lamb: 'the works of god are great and marvelous, and the ways of King of saints are just and true. Everybody shall fear you and praise your name because only you are godly and all tribes shall come and worship before you as your judgments are revealed.'

[John describes the Aegean sea in the evening setting sun. It appears like a sea of glass mingled with fire.
John describes a group-song scene: members of the choir are those who fought and overcome the beast and his number. The choir lined up before the throne and sang the song of Moses and of the Lamb with their god-supplied pocket-harps.]

RV.15: 5 Then the temple of the tent of the testimony in heaven was opened:

[Moses made a portable tent for God to sit and relax from the heat of the desert and called it the tent of testimony (Ex 38:21). Members of his tribe, the Levites, were declared the priestly caste and put in charge of this tent (Num 1:50; 17:7-8). God was made to sit on the lid of a wooden box guarding its contents which included the diary of Moses. To keep God motivated to sit on the lid of the box for ever, they placed some bread on a table in front of the box, at arm's length. It was called the 'show

bread' because God could see the bread but could not reach it and grab it and eat it. God sat there for ever hoping to get one day a piece of that tasty bread.
John's description 'the Temple of the tabernacle of the testimony' is redundant. Tabernacle means temple.]

RV.15: 6-7 The seven angels, wearing pure, white, linen clothes, with their breasts girded with golden girdles came out of the temple, carrying the seven plagues. One of the four beasts gave to the seven angels seven golden vials full of the wrath of immortal God.

[John refers to this particular god as the immortal (one who lives for ever) god. That means there are other gods who do not live for ever. John does not tell us specifically that Jesus is the man who sits on the throne. He gives enough hints to make the readers believe that he is Jesus. After reaching heaven, human beings will live for ever. That means human beings become immortal like that man who is sitting on the throne. The difference between immortal humans in heaven and the God who created the whole universe is that the creator has no beginning in addition to being immortal. Jesus was born to Mary, and therefore has a definite beginning and therefore is not god the creator.

According to Quran, god raised Jesus up to heaven. He will return to earth on the last day and die like all humans and will be resurrected again like all other creatures that lived on earth and he will judge all humans according to their deeds and send idol-worshippers and blasphemers, including Christians who call Jesus god, to hell-fire along with all other evil-doers.

Previously we were told that these seven angels were filled with the wrath of god; now they are given vials filled with the wrath of immortal god. If one of those angels trip and fall, the wrath of god from inside them and the wrath of god in the vial will spill and heaven will need a nasty cleanup job.]

RV.15: 8 The temple was filled with smoke from the brightness of God, and from his power and no man was able to enter into the temple, till the seven plagues of the seven angels were fulfilled.

[God cleared all the people out the temple with smoke that come from his brightness and from his power. Now, we know how he gets his brightness: he burns something that produces a lot of smoke. It would have been easier to use teargas to clear all the people out of the temple but that stuff was not yet invented.]

.

.

.

.

.

.

.

.

.

.

.

.

.

.

.

.

16 SEVEN VIALS POUREDON TO EARTH; PUNISHMENT OF BABYLON, BLASPHEMING BEAST; GATHERING IN ARMAGEDDON(RV.16)

RV.16: 1 A loud voice was heard out of the temple telling the seven angels: 'Go your ways and pour out the vials of the wrath of God upon the earth.'

[We will never know who gave this order: an angel or God himself? It came from the Temple of God in heaven. God was inside the temple. Because of the smoke emitting from his brightness, all the people ran out from the temple. So, God had the whole temple all for himself. At this time, if a loud voice came from the temple, it has to be that of God. Speaking of God, we do not know if it is the creator who has no beginning and no end or just an immortal god who has beginning but no ending.]

RV.16: 2-4 The first went and poured out his vial upon the earth. The men who had the mark of the beast and those who worshipped his image were afflicted with a serious foul sore. The second angel poured out his vial upon the sea. It became like the blood of a dead man and every living thing died in the sea. The third angel poured out his vial upon the rivers and fountains of waters. They became blood.

[John is plagiarizing some of the plagues which Moses used. Somebody might ask, if God could have done this by a verbal command instead of sending angels with vials? Couldn't America just drop few nuclear bombs in Iraq and Afghanistan and kill all their people instead of sending a large army and then torture and kill those people over longer period of time? Of course, yes. But low tech option is more suitable for winning the public opinion. Does God care about public opinion? Of course, yes. God is God only as long as somebody calls him God. If a tree fell in the forest and nobody heard it, did it really fall? Nobody calls Zeus 'God' any more. So, Zeus does not exist anymore. That is why God employs all these various teams of angels and saints and other good guys to constantly praise him in heaven and also on earth. God created this universe so that all his creations can praise him all the time. So, it is important to get the public opinion in his favor. Look what happened to his favorite people on earth. First they abandoned him and started thinking about fornication and murder all the time. Then he killed the whole world and kept only a small sample of good ones. From this good sample, he reared up 12 tribes who would be good to him. They invented the filthy Talmud and then stopped worshipping God and started worshipping Satan of Kabbalah. He sent Jesus to salvage them and bring them back to worshipping god of Moses. They killed Jesus. Then God killed a whole bunch of them in 70 AD and again in Kito's wars. Few remnants who believe in Jesus survived and some of them settled in Asia Minor near Patmos Island. God is trying to hold on to their worship and praise by doing the right thing. These old fashioned slow techniques like pouring out vials of wrath etc. will make him look just and patient in the eyes of people on earth and they might keep calling him God.]

RV.16: 5-6 I heard the angel of the waters say: 'you are righteous, O god, who is and was and shall be, because you have judged like this. Because they have shed the blood of saints and prophets and you have given them blood to drink; for they are worthy'.

[God gave blood to drink to those who slain the saints. That will teach them.]

RV.16: 7 Another voice out of the altar said: 'Even so, God Almighty, your judgments are true and righteous.'

[Public opinion is on the side of God.]

RV.16: 8-9 The fourth angel poured out his vial upon the sun and he was given power to scorch men with fire. Men were scorched with great heat. They blasphemed the name of God who has power over these plagues. They did not repent and praise him.

[The earth can be scorched by global warming which gradually raise temperature, or by solar flares and sun storms which can reach earth within minutes. In previous chapters sun and moon were darkened and one third of the sun and one third of the stars were destroyed etc. All those could have been temporary measures.]

RV.16: 10-11 The fifth angel poured out his vial upon the seat of the beast. And his kingdom was full of darkness and they chewed their tongues because of pain. They blasphemed the God of heaven because of their pains and their sores and did not repent of their deeds.

[The electric grid was hit this time. The beast's kingdom was thrown into darkness. But people who were already suffering from sores did not repent. They continued to blaspheme God.]

RV.16: 12 The sixth angel poured out his vial upon the great river Euphrates. Its water was dried up and riverbed became a highway for the kings of the East.

[Kings of East shall ride through the dried up riverbed to reach Armageddon to fight with God's army. Without water from Euphrates the population will die before Armageddon. The modern day Euphrates, Originates in eastern Turkey, and flows through Syria and Iraq and empties into the Persian Gulf. We cannot be sure if this Euphrates is the same Euphrates mentioned in Genesis or in Revelation.]

RV.16: 13-14 I saw three unclean spirits like frogs come out of the mouths of the dragon and the beast and the false prophet. They are the spirits of devils which work miracles and go forth to the kings of the earth and to the whole world, to gather them to the battle of that great day of God Almighty.

[The dragon finished chasing the woman and came back and the beast also came back after doing what it was supposed to do and the false prophet, we do not know where he came from, also came to the stage and they are all standing there with their mouths open. Then three frogs came out of their mouths. These frogs are spirits of the devil.

John says, these miracle working, unclean spirits of the devil are going to gather all the kings of the earth to battle with their creator, the God. People usually fight for wealth and for girls and the winners take it all. If God wins the battle, will he get the girls and the money?]

RV.16: 15 Look, I come as a thief. Those who are vigilant and keep their clothes with them are blessed because they may not walk naked and others won't see their shame.

[God says that he will come like a thief and take away everything they have got. Unless they are vigilant and keep their clothes with them while sleeping, they will have no clothes when they wake up and they will have to walk around naked and everybody will see their shameful urethral extension.

This verse is totally out of context and has no meaning in this context. May be this was a later interpolation!]

RV.16: 16 He gathered them together into a place called Armageddon in Hebrew.

[John says the unclean spirits in the form of frogs called the kings and their armies together into a place called Armageddon in Hebrew language. 'Armageddon' is not a Hebrew word or an Aramaic word or name of a place in any language anywhere in Middle East (the Biblical Universe). When writing a children's book, L. Frank Baum wondered what to call the place where the magical wizard lived. He looked at the encyclopedia volumes sitting in his book shelf. One the spine of one of the volumes was written 'O – Z' meaning that volume contained all the subject matters starting with letter 'O' to letter 'Z' in the alphabet. He got an idea: why not call the magical place OZ? He named his book 'The wonderful Wizard of OZ'. John, while writing his fictional story of a battle between God and Men, similar to the Greek mythology or epic of Mahabharata in India, he invented a place called Armageddon. In Mahabharata the epic battle between God and Devils took place in 'Kurukshetra'. John wrote 'Armageddon' is the Hebrew name. But, 'Armageddon' sounds more like a Greek word than a Hebrew word. That means John was a Greek. He did not know Hebrew or Aramaic. He was not a disciple of Jesus.]

RV.16: 17 The seventh angel poured out his vial into the air. A loud voice from the throne in the temple of heaven said: 'It is done'.

[Wait a minute, what happened when the seventh angel poured his vial? Nothing. Because a voice from the throne said 'it is over'. That was probably God who stayed further punishment. Who else can stop a vial full of wrath after it has been launched?]

RV.16: 18 There were voices and thunders and lightnings and a big earthquake, stronger than any earthquake since there were men on earth.

[John was standing in heaven. Did he feel this earth quake? Or, perhaps he saw the shaking of the earth from up there. If John was sitting in his cave writing, did the cave fall on him? Only God could tell if this was greatest quake since creation of man. Did God say that to John? Or, this was a figurative statement?].

RV.16: 19-20 The great city was split into three parts. The cities of the nations fell. God remembered to give great Babylon the cup of the wine of the fierceness of his wrath. Every island fled away and the mountains were not found.

[The earth cracked under the great city of Babylon (or, is it the great city of Jerusalem?) and it was split into three parts. The mountains were reduced to rubbles. The islands were covered over by tsunami water. John was definitely standing in heaven and watching all this.]

RV.16: 21 A big hail from heaven, each stone about the weight of a talent, fell on men. Men blasphemed God because the plague of hail was exceedingly great.

[People cursed God for dropping on them hail stones weighing up to 60 pounds. The only way John could be certain about what men on earth were saying is if God told him or if he made it up in his fantasy.]

17 WOMAN ON THE BEAST - MYSTERY BABYLON(RV.17)

RV.17: 1-2 One of the seven angels which had the seven vials came and told me: 'Come here. I will show you the judgment of the great whore that sits on many waters, with whom the kings of the earth have committed fornication, and the inhabitants of the earth have been made drunk with the wine of her fornication.'

[How can kings of the world make fornication (sexual intercourse) with the city of Babylon? Obviously this is a figurative statement referring to the many kings entering into treaties and agreements with Babylon. This is similar to America making treaties with Europe under the umbrella of NATO. Because of all the illegitimate wars they started since the formation of NATO, these agreements can be described as sinful treaties. John might write about America and the European countries thus: 'That harlot called USA with whom kings of Europe committed fornication.'

Inhabitants of the earth were made drunk with the wine of her fornication. That means the citizens of the countries which had treaties with Babylon became so arrogant because of their combined strength. In a modern day example, consider the tiny country Latvia. It even did not have an army. Then it became a member of NATO. Then Latvia became very bold and stood up to the giant Russia and started belligerence on their border. Tiny Latvia thinks nobody can touch it because it has a treaty with powerful America. John might write about the arrogance of Latvia based on its treaty with mighty USA (NATO) thus: 'Inhabitants of Latvia were made drunk with the wine of her fornication with USA.']

RV.17: 3 He carried me away in the spirit into the wilderness. And, I saw a woman sit on a scarlet colored beast with seven heads and ten horns and full of names of blasphemy.

[Blasphemy was written all over on this beast.]

RV.17: 4-5 The woman wore purple and red colored clothes, and gold and precious stones and pearls. In her hand she had a golden cup full of abominations and filthiness of her fornication. A name was written on her forehead: 'Mystery, Babylon the great, the mother of harlots and abominations of the earth.'

[In the modern world, America fits the description, because of all the criminal, unjust wars and plundering of the poor nations of the world. America is the mystery Babylon described in Revelation.]

RV.17: 6 I saw the woman drunken with the blood of the saints and with the blood of the martyrs of Jesus. When I saw her, I wondered with great admiration.

[According to john, the great city called 'mystery Babylon' has persecuted the believers in Jesus. The historic city of Babylon never mistreated Christians or any other religious group. It was a great tolerant, open-minded city, as far as we know. But this 'mystery Babylon' that exists only in the pages of Revelation apparently persecuted the believers in Jesus. Jews were the biggest persecutors of Christians and Muslims throughout history. Muslim religion requires that they protect Jews and Christians because they all believe in the same biblical stories. Hindus and Buddhists and other religions never persecuted anybody. They were all welcoming to other religions. But Jews killed Jesus and from the very beginning persecuted those who believed in Jesus. Even in modern times, the communists, who were actually Jews, killed 65 million Christians of Russia. The crypto-Jews (Jews who are outwardly Muslims) who ruled Turkey killed 1.5 million Armenian christians. Even today Jews continue to destroy Christianity through propagating homosexuality, immorality, pornography and secularism. So, the description of drinking blood of Christian martyrs fits modern day America which is fully under the control of the Jews who hate Jesus.]

RV.17: 7-8 The angel asked me: 'Why did you marvel? I will tell you the mystery of the woman and of the beast that carries her, which has the seven heads and ten horns. The beast that you saw was and is not and shall ascend out of the bottomless pit and go into perdition. Those earth-dwellers, whose names were not written in the book of life from the foundation of the world, shall be amazed when they see the beast that was and is not and yet is.

[A prophecy is not a prophecy unless it is couched in undecipherable riddles. Here John says that the people who were on earth at this time are those whose name was not written in the 'book of life' from the foundation of the world. When the foundation of the world was laid, god wrote down in the book of life, the names of all the people who will ever be created. Some people were not in the book. These are the Goyms (filthy animals). They were animals created in god's image but without souls (which means god did not blow into their nostrils), on the sixth day. They were the mud-people. They grew out of mud, like all animals and vegetation. Eastern European Jews call them 'goyms' and 'mud-people'. It is ironic because Eastern European Jews are themselves mud-people. They were nomads in Khazaria, today's Kazakhstan, until 10th century. Around 1000 AD, some of them converted to Talmudic Judaism and became Jews. They migrated to Eastern Europe and then later to other parts of Europe and to America. They are not descendants of Abraham. They are the mud-people who were created on the sixth day. Their calling other Goyms mud-people (or Goym) is ironic.

'The beast that was and is not and yet is' means the beast was alive but is dead now, but yet the beast is alive somewhere else.]

RV.17: 9-11 This is the clue. The seven heads are seven mountains on which the woman sits. And there are seven kings: five are fallen and one is and the other is not yet come. When he comes, he must continue for a short period. The beast that was and is not, is the eighth of the seven and goes into damnation.

[Here John gives us the clue to the riddle: 'woman sit on a red colored beast with seven heads and ten horns and full of names of blasphemy'. With this clue, everything will be as clear as La Brea Tar Pits. The seven heads of the beast represents seven mountains. That means the city of Babylon is sitting on seven mountains. Rome and Jerusalem both sit on seven hills. So, the mystery Babylon is eithr Rome or Jerusalem.

There are seven kings. In the description of the beast, there was seven heads but there were nothing else that was seven. So, what were these seven kings relating to? Of the seven kings, five are dead, the sixth one is still alive and the seventh one is not yet born, and when he is born he will live for a short period. Nobody has ever figured out who these kings or kingdoms are. John seems to be simply making things up to confuse the reader and make it look like some big mystery with deep meaning.

The beast is the eighth of the seven. Nobody has figured out this heavenly arithmetic. The beast is the eighth of the seven beasts and it goes into eternal damnation?]

RV.17: 12-14 And the ten horns which you saw are ten kings, which have received no kingdom as yet; but receive power as kings one hour with the beast. These have one mind, and shall give their power and strength to the beast. These shall make war with the Lamb, and the Lamb shall overcome them because he is god of gods and King of kings and those who are with him are called the chosen and the faithful.

[Nobody ever figured out what this means.]

RV.17: 15-17 The waters which you saw, where the whore sits, are peoples, and crowds, and tribes, and languages. The ten horns of the beast, shall hate the whore, and shall make her desolate and naked, and shall eat her flesh, and burn her with fire. Because God has put in their hearts to fulfill his will, and to agree, and give their kingdom to the beast, until the words of God shall be fulfilled.

[Here, John says that God has the power and ability to change people's hearts. If that is so, why not put some good thoughts into the minds of all people and make everybody good and take them all to heaven?]

RV.17: 18 The woman which you saw is that great city, which reigns over the kings of the earth.
[Thanks for explaining the 'mystery Babylon'. Now, at least John understands everything he wrote!]

18 JESUS DESTROYS BABYLON HUNDREDS OF YEARS AFTER IT WAS RUINED(RV.18)

RV.18: 1 Then I saw another angel who has great power come down from heaven. The earth was lightened with his brightness.

[John was standing in heaven talking to one of the seven angels with bottles full of anger of God (wrath). Then he saw another angel come down from heaven. So, this new angel came down from a higher heaven than the heaven he was standing on. So, there are several heavens – heaven on top of heaven. Quran says God created seven heavens. God is sitting in seventh heaven. Mohammed ascended up to seventh heaven and he saw bright lights which he understood as the veil of God and he heard a voice which he assumed was the voice of god or one of his secretaries and it came from behind the curtain. Muhammad explained that he did not see the man behind the curtain and nobody has. Bible says Moses saw the backside of God. Since Bible is extremely corrupt, can we believe Moses's statement that he saw the backside of God? Mohammed said god has no shape or form and he is unlike anything we can imagine. The voice from behind the curtain of light told Mohammed to pray five times. So, observant Muslims pray five times a day. Mohammed however prayed fifty times every day, even in the battlefield while fighting went on. If Quran, the uncorrupted book that came down from heavens, says there are seven heavens, it has to be true. So, this new angel whom John described came down from a higher heaven.]

RV.18: 2-3 He cried out in a loud voice: 'Babylon the great is fallen, is fallen, and is become the habitation of devils, and the hold of every foul spirit, and a cage of every unclean and hateful bird. Because all nations have drunk of the wine of the wrath of her fornication, and the kings of the earth have committed fornication with her, and the merchants of the earth have grown rich through the abundance of her delicacies.'

RV.18: 4-14 Another voice from heaven cried out: 'Come out of her, my people, so that you may not be partakers of her sins, so that you may not receive of her plagues. Because her sins have reached upto heaven, and God has remembered her sins. Reward her even as she rewarded you, and double to her double according to her works: in the cup which she hath filled fill to her double. How much she has praised herself, and lived deliciously, so much torment and sorrow give her: for she says in her heart, I sit a queen, and am no widow, and shall see no sorrow.

Therefore her plagues shall come in one day, death, and mourning, and famine; and she shall be utterly burned with fire because the God who judges her is strong.

The kings of the earth, who have committed fornication and lived deliciously with her, shall bewail her, and lament for her, when they shall see the smoke of her burning, standing afar off for the fear of her torment, saying: 'Alas, alas, that great city Babylon, that mighty city! Because your judgment came in one hour'.

The merchants of the earth shall weep and mourn over her. Because nobody buys their merchandise any more.

The merchandise of precious metals, precious stones, pearls, fine linen of vaious colors, precious wood, ivory, metals, marble, spices, perfume, ointments, fragrances, fine wine, oil, and flour, wheats, meats, animals, chariots, slaves, and men. Those precious and fine goods and fruits that you cherished are gone from you for ever.

[The second voice is reading out a very long press release. Usually when an anonymous voice is heard in heaven, it will be just one or two short sentences. This is a whole essay.]

RV.18: 15-19 'The merchants who became rich by selling these fine goods to you shall stand far away from torment of the city, weeping and wailing and saying: 'Oh that great city, which was clothed in fine linen, and purple, and scarlet, and decked with gold, and precious stones, and pearls! In one hour all those riches has come to nothing. All the crew of the merchant ships stood far away and cried when they saw the smoke of her burning, saying: 'Which other city is comparable to this great city!' They threw dust on their heads, crying, weeping and wailing, saying: 'Oh that great city in which all merchant ships made huge profits because of her high prices, is made desolate in one hour.' '

[In the middle of describing the great punishment of God on the great city of Babylon, John started talking in third person. So, this is not part of the original press release from heaven. This is a commentary by a third person reporter (John).]

RV.18: 20 Rejoice over her, you heaven, and you godly apostles and prophets because God took revenge on her for you.

[Babylon is the Greek name for the ancient Mesopotamian city on the banks of Euphrates called 'Bavillim' which in the ancient Akkadian language meant 'gate of God'. The story of the 'Tower of Bavel (confusion)' (Gen. 11) supposedly took place in the city of Babylon. Biblical Story tellers of Daniel, Jeremiah, and Isaiah located many of their stories in Babylon because it was a famous ancient city. The city had impregnable walls. It was a great seat of learning and culture. A great moral and legal code of law was developed there long before Moses came up with Ten Commandments. The 'Hanging Gardens of Babylon' was one of the seven wonders of ancient world.

Around 2334 BC, Sargon the Great became a famous ruler of Babylon. Around 1792 BC, Hammurabi became king and he united all of Mesopotamia into 'Babylonia'. Around 705 BC, Assyrian ruler Sennacherib destroyed the city. It was burned down and the ruins scattered. The apocalyptic fantasy adventure 'Revelation', describes the burning of Babylon as an example of what can happen to sinful cities. John took the event that happened 705BC and projected it into the future, near the end of times. The Revelation predicted the end of the world to happen soon after its writing, and thereby proved that is a fictional fantasy and not an inspired scripture.

King Esarhaddon re-built Babylon and returned it to its former glory. The city continued as a center of learning and culture. In 604 BC, Nebuchadnezzar II renovated the city and extended it. Herodotus wrote:

'The city stands on a broad plain, and is an exact square, a hundred and twenty stadia in length each way, so that the entire circuit is four hundred and eighty stadia. While such is its size, in magnificence there is no other city that approaches to it. It is surrounded, in the first place, by a broad and deep moat, full of water, behind which rises a wall fifty royal cubits in width and two hundred in height.' In the fantasy book Revelation, the new city of Jerusalem is built as a square with similar dimensions, except that in the fantasy Jerusalem, the height of the city walls is same as the length or width, making it a cube. Why would John make the walls of Jerusalem so high in heaven where there are no enemies or invaders? He also built it with a special kind if gold which is clear as glass. John further says: the 'tree of life' grows on the streets of this city made of solid gold and 'water of life' springs from the sold gold ground. John says the dead souls are invited to drink the water of life and eat the fruits of the tree of life. Even though John did not specifically say it, the reader can imagine what would happen after eating and drinking in heaven. The dead souls will poop somewhere and it will be solid gold. Hey, it is scripture and God's word!

Many ancient historians wrote about the great walls of Babylon as a wonder of the world. Nebuchadnezzar II built the Hanging Gardens of Babylon and Ishtar Gate. He also defeated Jews and brought some of them as captives to Babylon. Here, the corrupt and filthy rabbis wrote the filthy, vulgar, prejudiced, immoral 'Talmud' to circumvent the laws of Moses. Babylonian Talmud taught marrying and regular raping of three years old and even younger girls and homosexuality with boys 9 years and younger and lying to and cheating and swindling of Goym (non-Jews). Kabbalah which was developed alongside Talmud taught Satan-worship and child sacrifice etc. After some time, the captives went back to Palestine and rebuilt their temple and reestablished their community in Jerusalem. Hundreds of years after Babylon has disappeared from the face of earth, Jesus tried to rescue Jews from this Talmud and kabbalah and lost his life in the process.

Some stories featuring Babylonian King Belshazzar are in the Book of Daniel. In 539 BC, Cyrus the Great of Persia captured Babylon and made it their center of art and education. Mathematics, cosmology, and astronomy flourished. Thales of Miletus, the first western philosopher, studied there. Pythagoras developed his famous theorem based upon a Babylonian model. In 331 BC Alexander the Great, captured Babylon. By 141 BC, Babylon was deserted and forgotten.

Between 90 and 110 AD, John wrote his fantasy fiction called Revelation to spook the illiterate Asian Christians. According to john, Jesus took him to heaven and showed how God takes revenge on Babylon for the apostles and prophets etc. John did not know that Babylon did not mistreat apostles and saints and prophets. It was Jews who mistreated and killed all prophets and saints and apostles.

Christian apologists would say that the Babylon of Revelation is not the historic Babylon but a mystery Babylon. Mystery Babylon is a fictional fantasy city that exists in a parallel universe. But John did not know about parallel universes and he was specifically talking about historical Babylon that sat on many waters – Euphrates and Tigris.]

RV.18: 21 A mighty angel took up a stone like a large millstone, and threw it into the sea, saying: 'Like this the great city Babylon will be violently thrown down and it shall not exist anymore.'

[So, God is destroying a city that was covered up by desert hundreds of years ago. God is so powerful he can kill a city that vanished hundreds of years ago. Yet God is powerless against the New World Order crowd.]

RV.18: 22 And the voice of harpers, and musicians, and of pipers, and trumpeters, shall be heard no more at all in you; and no craftsman, of whatsoever craft he be, shall be found any more in you; and the sound of a millstone shall be heard no more at all in you;

RV.18: 23 And the light of a candle shall shine no more at all in you; and the voice of the bridegroom and of the bride shall be heard no more at all in you: for your merchants were the great men of the earth; for by your sorceries were all nations deceived.

RV.18: 24 And in her was found the blood of prophets, and of saints, and of all that were slain upon the earth.

[Children of Jacob were always jealous of the ancient civilizations of Egypt and Babylon, because they had their own Laws and Gods and history and civilization long before there was a One God and his favorite people and Moses and his commandments. So they always wrote bad things about these ancient civilizations. The Babylonians defeated and captured the children of Jacob and took them to Babylon and gave them some civilization before sending them back to build their temple in Jerusalem. After that the hatred towards Babylon increased tenfold. John the Greek Jew hated Jesus because he tried to bring Jews back to laws of Moses from filthy Babylonian Talmud which tell Rabbis to marry and regularly rape 3 year old Jewish (and even younger than three year old non-Jewish) girls and practice pedophilia and homosexuality with boys under nine years and lie to and cheat non-Jews and confiscate their property, etc. When John wrote the spoof called the 'Revelation' to fool and make fun of gullible Christians, he described the fall of Babylon which happened a millennia ago as the future event. The Christian peasants who knew nothing about these ancient Babylon believed it all as the future event of end of times. In this chapter John describes a fictional fall of Babylon.]

.

.

.

.

.

.

.

19 BATTLE BETWEEN JESUS AND BEAST AND FALSE PROPHET (RV.19)

RV.19: 1-2 Then I heard a loud voice of many people in heaven: 'Alleluia; Salvation, and fame and honor and power to our God: because his judgments are true and righteous. Because he has judged the great whore, which corrupted the earth with her fornication, and has avenged the blood of his servants at her hand.

[Long before John wrote this, Babylon has declined and fell into ruin. There has never been any religious persecution in Babylon. But it is true that Jewish Rabbis became big-time fornicators and pedophiles and homosexuals and child molesters and whoremongers while they lived in Babylon and they codified all their filthy criminal immorality into 'Babylonian Talmud'. Decline and fall of Babylon was not a wrath of God. Instead it was a natural historical process just like the decline of Egyptian, Persian, Roman, British, French and Spanish empires and soon American empire.]

RV.19: 3-4 Again they said: 'Alleluia'. And her smoke rose up for ever and ever. The twenty four elders and the four beasts fell down and worshipped God that sat on the throne, saying: 'Amen; Alleluia'.

['Alleluia' is the Greek rendering of the words 'ya Allahu' (oh God). 'Allahu' means God in the Aramaic, the language of Jesus and also in Arabic, the language of Ishmael, the first son of Abraham and his descendants. 'Ella', 'Ello' and 'Alla' are the Hebrew word for God. 'Ya' in Aramaic is equivalent to 'oh' in English. When the words 'Ya Allahu' is repeated in rapid succession while praising God, it becomes like: 'Ya Allahu, ya Allahu, ... ya allahu ya, allahu ya, allahu ya... allahuya, allahuya, allahuya,... alleluia alleluia..' John rendered this in Greek as 'Alleluya'. In today's world, Christians keep singing 'Alleluya' without knowing the origins of that expression.]

RV.19: 5 A voice came out of the throne: 'Praise our God, all you his servants, and you that fear him, both small and great'.

[Did God tell everybody to worship God? Or, did one of the beasts tell everybody to worship God? The throne is full of beasts and dead lamb and eternal man and other things and creatures. Thunder and lightning and hail and smoke come out of it all the time signifying that God is sitting on it. Throne is like a perpetual fireworks stand and heavy-metal concert stage. So, who made this pronouncement from the throne? Perhaps, the throne itself spoke. It is possible.]

RV.19: 6-8 Then I heard the voice of a large crowd, like crashing waves and great thunders: 'Alleluia, because the omnipotent God reigns. Let us be glad and rejoice and honor him. Because the marriage of the Lamb is come and his wife has made herself ready. She was ordained to be clothed in fine, clean, white linen. Because the fine linen is the righteousness of saints.'

RV.19: 9 And he told me: 'Write: those who are called to the marriage supper of the Lamb are Blessed. These are the true sayings of God'.

[He told John. He, Who? Did Jesus tell John to write that the invitees are blessed? Does that mean, they will get more sheep and goat and wives and children?
Jesus told John that these are true words of God, meaning, some other words are not true words of God.]

RV.19: 10 I fell at his feet to worship him. He told me: 'don't do it. I am your fellow servant and of your brethren that have the testimony of Jesus. Worship God, because the testimony of Jesus is the spirit of prophecy'.

[Here, John is recycling an incident from *'(Acts 10:25-26). When Peter came in, Cornelius met him, and fell down at his feet, and worshipped him. But Peter took him up, saying: 'Stand up; I myself also am a man.'*

While Jesus was alive, he never forbade anybody from worshipping him. If the author of 'Revelation' was a disciple of Jesus, he would have known that.

Worship God (the father) because the statement of Jesus is the spirit of prophecy. Does that mean Jesus has the ability to prophecy?]

RV.19: 11-13 Then I saw heaven opened, and the one who is called 'Faithful and True, and righteous judge and war maker' sat on a white horse. His eyes were like flame of fire, and many crowns were on his head; and he had a name written, that no man knew, but he himself. And he was clothed with vesture dipped in blood: and his name is: 'The Word of God'.

[John was standing in heaven talking. Then heaven above them opened. Then 'The word of God' (Is this Jesus?) appeared sitting on a horse. He had his name written on a name tag, which only he could read. John read the name which no man can read and it is: 'The Word of God'. On his head was a bunch of crowns and he was wearing a cloak dipped in blood and his eyes were burning flame.]

RV.19: 14 The armies which were in heaven, clothed in fine, white, clean linen, followed him on white horses.

[Is it possible for angels to mount heavenly horses and go for battle with enemy? There is a well-documented and corroborated incident in which angels fought with humans:
"In the battle of Badr, Prophet Mohammed prayed humbly to God to help his small rag-tag army against the well-armed large fighting force of Meccans. God sent angels down. During the battle when the Muslims heard that Kuzar Bin Jabbir, a prominent tribal leader was coming to help the Meccans with a greater force, Allah also increased the support to His followers.

'O Muhammad,... Allah helped you at the Battle of Badr when you were helpless. .. Remember when you said to the believers, 'Is it not enough that Allah should send down three thousand angels to help you?' Of course! If you remain patient and on your guard, Allah will send to your aid not three thousand but, five thousand specially marked angels in case of a sudden attack from the enemy'. (Quran, Ali Imran, (3: 123-125))

After embracing Islam, Saib Bin Jabesh, describing the incident of his arrest said: 'I was running away with the idolaters when a tall young man came in front of me riding a spotted horse. He grabbed me so strongly that I could not move, and then he tied me with a rope. In the meantime Abdur Rahman Bin Auz came to me and shouted: 'Whose captive is this?' When nobody replied he took me to The Holy Prophet & presented my case. The Holy Prophet asked me: 'Who had captured you?' I remained silent, because I didn't want to tell anything. Then The Holy Prophet himself stated that I had been captured by the Angel of God. He then said to Abdur Rahman, 'Oh Abdur Rahman, take him away, he is now your prisoner'.

An Ansari said: 'Oh Prophet, I was following an idolater to kill him, but he was quite ahead of me, Suddenly I felt a rider overtaking me & I heard the rider saying 'Aqdim Ya Haizoom', a moment later I saw the head of that infidel lying on the ground, I ran & picked him up'. Prophet Mohammed said 'Haizoom' is the name of Angel Gabriel's horse. He was helping you in the battle field.

Abbas Bin Abdul Mutalib who was quite tall was arrested by Abu-l-Yaseer Kaab Bin Amr. Prophet Mohammed inquired Hazrat Abu-l-Yaseer, 'How did you capture him?' He replied: 'A total stranger helped me capture him. He had a dignified personality & was riding on a spotted horse'. The Holy Prophet said 'Oh Abu-l-Yaseer, the person who helped you was one of the Angels of God who had descended to help in Battle of Badr'.

Abu Sufyaan told the story of the battle to Abu Laheb & other idolaters: 'The Muslims were great in number & there was no scarcity of arms & ammunitions. We also saw among them people having white faces, wearing white dresses & turbans, riding on spotted horses. They never missed their aim whenever they attacked our friends. They flew between the heaven & the earth; we could never compete with them.' "]

RV.19: 15 Out of his mouth goes a sharp sword, with which should strike the tribes and he shall rule them with an iron rod and he treads the winepress of the fierceness and anger of Almighty God.

[So, this man from heaven is not God. But, he could be Jesus. He is going to strike down the tribes with the sword in his mouth. Probably John saw a snake flickering its long tongue before striking a prey. John took the analogy of a snake with its long forked tongue and made up the image of a man with a sword stuck in his mouth. In the first chapter, Jesus had a sword sticking out of his mouth.

People wonder why Jesus is going to rule the world with a rod of iron. In the olden days kings used to carry a stick. King used to beat his servants or followers with it. Then kings became emperors and rich and they started decorating the stick with gold and precious stones etc. Gold in its pure form was available on the surface of earth in many places and is very soft and can be easily made into a rod. Iron was rare in its pure form on surface of earth. Plus iron was hard and difficult to form into any shape. So, iron was a rare precious commodity. John lists iron among precious metals and stones that were brought to Babylon by merchants. In the mid 19-th century, *aluminum was more valuable than gold. Aluminum cutlery was given to honored guests to eat with in Napoléon III's dinners. Fashionable women wore aluminum jewelry.*
After WWII, the US government decided to honor General Patton with a medal made of aluminum which was the most precious metal on earth at that time. According to John, Jesus will rule the tribes with a staff made of iron, which was the most precious metal of the time.

Quran describes iron as the metal of great strength forged in outer space. Quran also states that human body will disintegrate into its components including iron. (At that time, nobody knew iron was part of blood). Modern science tells us that iron is formed in the center of huge stars, thousands of times bigger than sun. So, Jesus will rule his world with a rod of precious metal iron. Many modern preachers think iron rod represent an iron fist and powerful laws. Strength or power of the king does not come from the strength of his staff which is mostly ceremonial and decorative. Otherwise, the queen of England would have been holding a massive staff made of tungsten.]

RV.19: 16 On his coat and on his thigh a name is written: ‘King of Kings and God of Gods’.

[Previously it was told that Jesus walked around with a name tag which no humans could read (except John, of course.) Now, this guy is walking around with labels that read 'King of kings and God of gods', stuck to his over coat and also to his thigh. Does that mean this creature is God the creator, or does that mean he is rooting for God the creator? Oh, the labels had to be in Greek, because that is the only language John could read. So, the question becomes: 'is God the creator a Greek god?' If the label is visible on his thigh he must be walking around practically naked from waist down. Was he wearing a thong and a half-coat or was he completely naked from his waist down?]

RV.19: 17-18 I saw an angel standing in the sun. He cried out to all the birds that fly in the middle of heaven: 'Come, gather together for the supper of the great God, so that you may eat the flesh of kings and captains and mighty men and horses, and their riders and the flesh of all men, both free and bonded, both small and big.'

[So, an angel standing in the sunlight called out all the birds that fly above, to gather together to eat a great dinner provided by Great God (God the father, the creator). Flesh of men of all walks and sizes and horses are to be served. John was standing in heaven and looking down on earth.]

RV.19: 19-21 I saw the beast, and the kings of the earth, and their armies, gathered together to make war against the one that sat on the horse and his army. He who sat on the horse, took the beast and the false prophet that made miracles before him, with which he deceived those who had the mark of the beast and those who worshipped his image, and threw them into the lake of fire burning with brimstone. The remnant were slain with the sword which proceeded out of his mouth. All the birds ate their flesh.

[So, the man on the horse with a sword for a tongue captured both the beast and the miracle-working false-prophet and threw them into the lake of fire and killed their armies.]

20 DEVIL LOCKED UP, RESURRECTION OF 144000 JEWS, THOUSAND YEAR REIGN OF JESUS IN HEAVEN, RESURRECTION OF GOYM, GOYM AND DEATH AND HELL THROWN INTO LAKE OF FIRE (RV.20)

RV.20: 1 An angel carrying the key of the bottomless pit and a long chain in his hand came down from heaven.

[John has seen gladiator fights on the Patmos Island. Here, John is describing a heavenly gladiator fight. John was standing in the heaven. Billions of angels and 144000 singing chorus and the 24 elders of unknown origin, and the four beasts with eyes everywhere and inside and the dead goat and the immortal man and the tens of thousands of martyrs slain for their faith, billions of dead goym with palm leaves in their hands are all sitting or standing like in a Roman coliseum. Then an angel came down from the second heaven, and entered the arena, like a gladiator, with key to the bottomless pit and a chain. The opponent will be let loose and the gladiator will slay the opponent and everybody will enjoy the show.]

RV.20: 2-3 He caught the dragon, that old serpent, which is the Devil and Satan. He tied him up and threw him into the bottomless pit and shut him up for a thousand years and set a seal on him, so that he cannot deceive the tribes until thousand years have completed and after that he must be loosed for a little while.

RV.20: 4 The souls of those who were beheaded for the witness of Jesus and for the word of God, sat on thrones. They had not worshipped the beast or his image, and they had not received his mark on their foreheads or in their hands. Judgment was given to them. They lived and reigned with Christ a thousand years.

[So, the angel from second heaven tied up Satan and locked him up in the bottomless pit for thousand years and put a seal, which is equivalent to a time lock. Then the martyrs who were killed for their faith in Jesus were put on thrones and they reigned with Jesus 1000 years. So the thousand year reign of Jesus is taking place in heaven. John stood there in heaven and watched this thousand year reign. It was easy because time flies when you are in heaven (or, when you are seeing a vision).]

RV.20: 5 This is the first resurrection. The rest of the dead would not be resurrected until the thousand years were finished.

[This was a private closed door resurrection event by invitation only for the martyrs. Another resurrection for the general public will be scheduled 1000 years from now, when Satan is brought out.]

RV.20: 6 Those who are part of the first resurrection are Blessed and godly in that the second death has no power on them, and they shall be priests of God and of Christ, and shall reign with him a thousand years.

RV.20: 7-8 At the end of thousand years, Satan shall be loosed out of his prison, and shall go out to deceive the tribes which are in the four quarters of the earth, namely Gog of Magog, to gather them together to battle. They will be as numerous as the sand of the sea.

[After 1000 year reign of Jesus and his beheaded martyrs who were resurrected in a private resurrection event, the Satan will be released from his prison, the bottomless pit. During the 1000 year reign of Jesus in heaven, people continued their lives on earth. The Satan will go out and try to deceive the people in four corners of the world, which is the land of Magog headed by their leader Gog. During the 1000 years when Satan was absent from the world, the people of the land of Magog multiplied abundantly and became numerous like the sand of the sea. According to (Ezekiel 38:1-9), Satan will gather them together for battle against children of Jacob. According to John's Revelation, they will be gathered together for battle against Jesus.]

RV.20: 9-10 They went up on the breadth of the earth, and surrounded the camp of the saints and the beloved city. Fire came down from God out of heaven, and consumed them. The devil that deceived them was cast into the lake of fire and sulfur, where the beast and the false prophet are, and shall be tormented day and night for eternity.

[John stood there in heaven and watched the whole battle that happened on earth and its final conclusion.]

RV.20: 11 I saw a large white throne, and the one who sat on it. The earth and the heaven went away from in front of him and no place was found for them.

[The heaven and earth just passed away. But the seas did not pass away. Because seas are separate from earth and heaven. Seas are eternal. In the beginning the spirit of god hovered over the waters. Then the earth rose up from the sea.]

RV.20: 12-15 The dead of all sizes stood before God; and the book of life was opened. The dead were judged according to their works as written in the books. The sea gave up the dead who were in it; and death and hell delivered up the dead which were in them. And death and hell were thrown into the lake of fire. This is the second death. Whosoever was not found written in the book of life was thrown into the lake of fire.

[So, everything that everybody does in his lifetime is written in books in heaven. Those who died in water will be resurrected from sea. Those who were held by death and by hell were resurrected from them. Evil doers are taken to hell immediately after death for punishment. Others will be held by death in a state of death. They will all be resurrected and judged according to what is written in the books in heaven. Those 'soul-less animals' in human form, called the Goym, would not have their names written in the book of life. They will not be judged. At the end of the judgment process, the Goym along with death and hell will be tossed out into the lake of fire and sulfur. After this event, there won't be any more death and hell. John stood there in heaven and watched all this final judgment process.

Hell is separate from lake of fire. Hell is where sinners are punished in accordance with their crimes. Hell is like the secret CIA prisons where Muslims are tortured and water boarded endlessly. When they die from torture, they will be revived by Israeli trained doctors and then tortured again. Lake of fire is like a furnace which indiscriminately burns everything in it for ever. Since souls and angels cannot die, they will be burned for eternity.

Prophet Mohammed also talked about the books in heaven. When he was raised to seventh heaven, he heard the pens writing everything behind the curtain. Quran talks about this book: 'There are two (receivers) listening, one on the right and one on the left'(Quran, Qaf (50:17)). And every small and great thing they did is written down. (Quran, Al-Qamar (54:52-53) We bring the dead to life and have written down all things in a clear register. (Quran,Ya-Sin (36:12))

On day of Judgment, the record of their deeds shall be opened. And they shall find all that they did placed before them and your God shall not be unjust to anyone."(Quran, Al-Kahf (18:48-49))]

.

.

.

.

.

.

.

.

.

.

.

21 NEW HEAVEN AND NEW EARTH; WEDDING OF LAMB AND THE CITY; NEW PRE-FAB CITY MADE IN SECOND HEAVEN DESCENDS TO NEW EARTH (RV.21)

RV.21: 1 I saw a new heaven and a new earth. The first heaven and the first earth were passed away. And there was no more sea. I, John, saw the holy city, New Jerusalem, coming down from God out of heaven, prepared as a bride adorned for her husband.

[The first earth and heaven and the sea were moved out and a new earth and a new heaven (but no sea) were moved into place. John could be describing what happened after a major eruption in his neighboring 'Thera' island. The old island and sea were all replaced by new lava and it solidified into a new land and there was no sea visible from his vantage point from the Psili Ammos beach. Later a glimpse of sunrays shone through the thick dark smoke filled atmosphere. John interpreted it as the New Jerusalem being lowered down from heaven into the new lava earth.

Quran also talks about a new earth and a new heaven. *"Then, with one blast of the horn, the earth and the mountains will be crushed. On that Day, the Resurrection will occur, and the heaven will split open." (Quran (69:13-16)).*

"On that day, the earth and heavens will be replaced by new earth and new heavens. And all creatures will come out before the one and only God. On that day, the sinners will be bound together in shackles." (Quran (14:48-49)).

A new holy city was decorated for inauguration, like a bride is prepared for her husband, and lowered from heaven into the new earth without seas.]

RV.21: 3-4 A loud voice was heard from heaven: 'Look, the tent of God is among men. He will live with them and they shall be his people. God himself shall be with them and he will be their God. And God shall wipe away all tears from their eyes. There shall be no more death or sorrow or crying or pain. Because the former things are passed away'.

[So, John ends his book on a positive note with hope for future. God lowered a new tent (Ref. Exodus) into the new earth inhabited entirely by resurrected people who were judged to be worthy. There shall be no death and disease and sorrow. All those things were from the previous earth and heaven. Since he could not think of a good way to put it, John borrowed the words from (Leviticus 26:11-12), (Exodus 6:7) and (Jeremiah 30:22): 'And God will live among his new people for ever in his brand spanking new decked-out tent, called 'tabernacle' in Hebrew, proudly made by angels in second heaven, and he shall be their god.'

Did god zap the free will of the people before deciding to live among them? If not, they may go astray and God will not be able to kill them again because death was burned up in the lake of fire.]

RV.21: 5 The one who sat on the throne said: 'Look, I make all things new'. He told me: 'Write. Because these words are true and faithful'.

[The one who sat on the throne is God the father (who else can make everything new) or Jesus. God (or Jesus) said: 'write because these words are true and faithful'. That means usually his words are not true and faithful, but this time it is different. This time he is truthful and faithful! Now, one question: what does faithful mean? Faithful to whom?]

RV.21: 6-8 Then, he told me: 'It is done. I am Alpha and Omega, the beginning and the end. I will give the fountain of the water of life freely to those who thirst. He who overcomes shall inherit all things; and I will be his God, and he shall be my son. But the fearful, and unbelieving, and the abominable, and murderers, and whoremongers, and sorcerers, and idolaters, and all liars, shall have their part in the lake which burns with fire and brimstone: which is the second death'

[That was a nice speech by God (or Jesus).
For good men, there is only one death. The bad men will die twice.
Burning in lake of fire for ever is the second death.

According to Quran, two deaths are ordained for all souls. When a soul desire to be born as a man, he is given death and then given birth again in a human body. Then that soul will die again and will be resurrected on the day if judgment in reconstituted body. Thus everybody experience two deaths and two births. Then they will either be confined to heaven or to hell fire for eternity.]

RV.21: 9 One of the seven angels which had the seven vials full of the seven last plagues came to me and said: 'Come here, I will show you the bride, the Lamb's wife.'

[Every good story book ends with the wedding of the hero and the beautiful princess and then they will live happily ever after. The end. John is ending his story book with the wedding of the slain lamb with seven heads and several horns with the mystery bride.]

RV.21: 10 He carried me away in the spirit to a big and tall mountain, and showed me that great city, the holy Jerusalem, descending out of heaven from God, with the brightness of God, clear as crystal, shining like a Jasper stone.

[John did not know that Jasper is an opaque rock of virtually any color. John made his New Jerusalem city a shining crystal clear opaque rock! When he saw it, it was still descending slowly, like the heaven was giving birth to this rock.]

RV.21: 12-13 It had a big, tall wall with twelve gates, three on each of the sides. Each gate had a name corresponding to one of the twelve tribes of Jacob written on it, and was guarded by an angel.

[This is new world and new heaven, with no sea, no death, no sorrow, no bad people, no wants. Who are these angels guarding the gates against? Are they trying to protect the holy city from stray angels? Obviously the author did not think everything through before writing all these nonsense. He makes it look like somebody might steal it away or something.]

RV.21: 14 The wall of the city had twelve foundations, and in them the names of the twelve apostles of the Lamb.

[This new holy city is pre-fabricated in second heaven and slowly lowered to the new earth without sea and new heavens. It has 12 gates named after 12 tribes, even though 10 of those tribes have been lost, and now it has 12 foundations each named after one of 12 disciples, even though one was son of perdition.

The Lamb had 12 disciples. That implies that the Lamb is Jesus. Until now the readers thought Jesus was the immoral man on the throne, the creature with a sword sticking out of its mouth, and the man on the horse with a sword sticking out his mouth, etc. May be these are all body doubles of Jesus.]

RV.21: 15-18 The angel who talked to me had a golden stick to measure the city and its walls and its gates. The length and breadth and height of the city are twelve thousand furlongs each. The wall was built with Jasper and measured hundred forty four cubits. The city was pure gold, like clear glass.

[The number 144 is important. Each side is 12 tribes x 12 times (144) cubits. That is enough to house 12 tribes x 12 times x 1000 descendants of Jacob. (In heaven, souls are highly compressed). It is an engineering marvel because the city is a cube shape and each of the length and breadth and height measures 12 tribes x 1000 furlongs. (1 furlong is 220 feet). But the walls surrounding it measures only 12 tribes x 12 cubits (1 cubit =18 inches). How does that work? Human calculations cannot figure it out. Only heavenly engineering and John's fantasy and fixation with 12 tribes can make it happen. It is obvious that John was throwing some measures like cubit and furlongs and some 12's to represent twelve tribes and 12 disciples and 1000's to make things sound big, without thinking through what would it all look like when put together.]

RV.21: 19-26 And the foundations of the wall of the city were garnished with all manner of precious stones. The twelve gates were twelve pearls; the street of the city was pure gold, and looked like transparent glass. There was no temple in it because God Almighty and the Lamb are its temple. The city had no need of the sun or moon, as the brightness of God and of Lamb would light it. The tribes that are saved shall walk in its light and the kings of the earth bring their brightness and honor into it. Its gates shall not be shut at end of day because there shall be no night there. They shall bring the brightness and honor of the tribes into it.

[This is all just mindless fantasy like in a video game. Foundations of a heavenly building? The whole city, for 144000 plus souls, is built on 12 layers of foundattions, and these foundations which go below the grade (underground) are garnished with precious stones! Stones are considered precious because they are rare. Are these stones rare in heaven? Are the souls in the market for stones? If nobody is in the market for stones, will they be precious? Well, Jesus showed it to John, John wrote it, we believe it and that settles it!]

RV.21: 27 Nothing that defiles or cause abomination or make lie shall enter it; only those who are written in the Lamb's book of life shall enter it.

[Duh! In the new earth and heaven there are only the 144000 plus resurrected dead people. The rif-raf were all burned up in the lake of fire. So, there is nothing in heaven that can cause defilement.]

.

.

.

.

.

.

.

.

.

22 RIVER OF LIFE; TREE OF LIFE; THRONE OF GOD AND THRONE OF LAMB(JESUS); JESUS PROMISES TO JOHN TO COME QUICLY AND TO BLESS THOSE WHO BELIEVE THIS BOOK; FINAL CURSES AND BLESSINGS *(RV.22)*

RV.22: 1 He showed me a pure river of water of life, clear as crystal, proceeding out of the throne of God and of the Lamb.

[In a stable or cow shed, there is always urine on the floor. May be this stream originating from the throne is the pee of the eternal man, the dead lamb, the weird beasts and the god-knows-what-else that crowds the throne.]

RV.22: 2 In the middle of the street of the city, and on either side of the river, there were 'tree of life', which bare twelve kinds of fruits, every month. The leaves of the trees were medicine for the tribes.

[In new earth and heaven, with no seas, and only one stream with clear water and people with no diseases and no worries and no death, trees of life grew in the middle of the street in the city and on either side of the stream. Twelve types of fruits grew on those trees year round (12 months) for resurrected dead people, who do not eat, to eat and the leaves of the trees were medicinal treatment of the tribes who never get sick!]

RV.22: 3-4 There shall be no more curses. But the throne of God and of the Lamb shall be in it and his servants shall serve him. They shall see his face and his name shall be in their foreheads.

[Men who live on earth cannot see God. Those who live in heaven can see God. Everybody in heaven shall have the name of God written on their forehead. If everybody has the same name tag, what purpose would it serve?]

RV.22: 5 There shall be no night there and they do not need sun light or candle or light because God gives them light and they shall live for ever.

[Sun and moon were darkened. So there is no light in heaven. The concepts of electric lights, street lighting etc. were unknown to John. The technology of heaven is only as advanced as what John knows. So, the whole heaven is in perpetual darkness. Thank God, the lamb and the god and the saints, and martyrs are all fluorescent. They emit their own light and it lights up the whole heaven. If they were not fluorescent, the angels and 144000 saved souls etc. would all be groping in darkness like blind men.]

RV.22: 6-7 He told me: 'These sayings are faithful and true. The God of the godly prophets sent his angel to show to his servants the things which must shortly be done. Look, I come quickly. Those who keep the prophecy of this book are blessed.'

[So, the angel who was showing John the bride of the dead Lamb told John that 'these sayings (which John wrote in his book of Revelations) are faithful and true. The God of Prophets sent his angel (the weird creature with a sword sticking out of his mouth seen in the opening chapter) to show his servant John the things which will happen shortly. Then either the angel who is talking to John now, or God himself, says, that he will come shortly (hopefully, not before John finish writing).

This is the second time God has personally stuck his neck out and certified the truthfulness of this book! God also told John that whoever keep the sayings in this book will be blessed, which coming from God means that they will get more wives, children, slaves, sheep and goat. Blessings usually come with curses. So, you can be sure God will soon curse those who do not keep the sayings in this book.]

RV.22: 8 I, John, saw these things, and heard them. Then I fell down to worship before the feet of the angel which showed me these things.

[Here, John is affirming that the author is John and that he heard and seen the things written in this book. This book is not fiction or scam like many other books that were written in those days (first century). John was so overwhelmed by all these visions, he fell down on his face in front of the angel to worship him. That was the standard practice of worshipping in those days.]

RV.22: 9 Then he told me: 'Do not do it. Because I am your fellow servant, and of your brethren the prophets, and of them which keep the sayings of this book. Worship God.'

[Previously John tried to worship Jesus and he told him the same thing. Now, Angel is telling John to worship god. This is the second use of this plagiarized scene.]

RV.22: 10-16 He told me: 'Do not seal the prophecies of this book: because the time is at hand. Let people continue to be the way they are – unjust, filthy, righteous or holy. Look, I come quickly; and my reward is with me, which I shall give to every man according to his work. I am Alpha and Omega, the beginning and the end, the first and the last. Those who do his commandments shall have the right to the tree of life, and may enter the city through the gates. Because, dogs, and sorcerers, and whoremongers, and murderers, and idolaters, and whosoever loves and makes a lie. I, Jesus, have sent my angel to tell you to tell these things in the churches. I am the root and the offspring of David and the bright morning star.'

[Now, Jesus has put his seal of authenticity on this book. He sent his angel to tell John to tell the churches these things. Which Christian can question a direct order from Jesus? It is interesting that Jesus says his authority comes from the fact that he is the root and offspring of David. So, David is the big boss, the real McCoy. What about all that talk in the Gospels about Jesus being born miraculously without a father? If he was born without a father, that would make him NOT-the-offspring-of-David, wouldn't it? The Bible does not say that Jesus is the root of David. Root is the genealogical root. David's or anybody else's root can only be another human being. Jesus is not mentioned as the root of David. May be the writer meant that God created Adam and all humans are descendants of Adam. In that case God is the root, not Jesus. Jesus was created by God; that is why Jesus prays to God in heaven, his creator. May be the writer meant that God the creator created Jesus first and then sent Jesus to create Adam. Bible clearly says that God the creator created Adam, not another person or agent of God. The idea that Jesus was created before the world originated came long after the death of Jesus. Jesus never said he was there before the world was created. Jesus never said that he was a word and then word became flesh etc. Mary and his brethren (family members) treated Jesus like any other member of their family. Mary never prayed to Jesus as her creator. None of the disciples worshipped Jesus as their creator. If Jesus was the creator, then, would he sneak into the sex organ of poor teen Mary and then hide there for nine months spying on her and then come out? What kind of perverted kinky god would do such a foul thing? Oh well, John says Jesus said it, we believe it and that settles it!]

RV.22:17-20 The Spirit and the bride say: 'Come. Let those who can hear, come. Let those who are thirsty, come. Let those who come take the water of life freely. Because I testify to every man that hears the prophecies of this book: If anybody shall add to these things, God shall add to him the plagues that are written in this book. If any man shall take away from the prophecies of this book, God shall take away his name out of the book of life, and out of the holy city, and from the things which are written in this book. He who testifies these things says: 'Surely I come quickly. Amen. Even so, come, Lord Jesus.'

[The spirit (angel who was showing John the bride of the dead lamb) and bride (the prefabricated heavenly city of Jerusalem that descended from second heaven in the shape of a cube of 600x600x600 furlongs) together sent verbal invitation to all those who can hear, to come and drink the water of life free of charge. Unfortunately, the only people who can hear the Lamb and the cube are John and may be a couple of angels who are standing nearby. And they are not thirsty.

Are they (Lamb and the cube) authorized to invite men living on earth to go and drink the water of life which is flowing in a stream in the new Holy city made of gold and Jasper that was lowered from the second heaven to the new earth? The inhabitants of the earth have already been killed off. The sun and moon darkened. The earth and heavens passed away. At this point there are no human beings around to hear this announcement.

The only people who shall ever enter the new earth are the 144000 plus dead people mostly from the twelve tribes of Jacob. There are angels guarding the gates of this city and won't let any man enter unless they have the name of God written on their forehead. John did not tell us what the name of God was. Did he know?

The Lamb and cube team put a curse on those who would add or subtract words from this book. Are they authorized to remove the name of someone from the book of life?
Then Jesus promise to come quickly.
Jesus said 'Amen'! Real Jesus would never have done that. Then John added his prayer, 'even so, come soon Jesus'. He was talking to Jesus. Now he is praying to Jesus to come soon.]

RV.22: 21 The grace of our Lord Jesus Christ be with you all. Amen.

[So, finally John blessed his audience, the Asian Christians. He obviously is authorized by Jesus to distribute the grace (blessing) of Jesus to whomever he pleases: in this case, his audience. Then he also said 'amen'. That is like saying 'the end'.

In the vision of John, the issues that bother God at the end of the world are contemporary Jewish persecution of Christians. The world powers are Rome and Syrians and Babylonians and other regional small time players of the time. All the weapons and transportation and war tactics are those that prevailed in his time. America, China, Russia, Australia, India and Africa are not mentioned. Some of the strange creatures mentioned may be airplanes, rockets, tanks, warships, satellite communications, nuclear bombs and robots. God is trying to overcome the world and the devil and death! The great world powers met in a fictitious location near Jerusalem. In his second coming, Jesus came down from heaven on the wings of some birds. Battle is directed through blowing of trumpets.

The book says it is prophecy of God. A prophecy is judged as a prophecy if what was said happens. Nothing mentioned in this book ever happened. So this is not a prophecy.

The Asians had no way of validating the book. They didn't want to take a chance with the so-called words or Jesus and the promised blessings and curses written in the book. So they believed it. 225 years later, when the Nicaea conference rolled around, somebody carried this book to Nicaea. The attendees of the conference failed to notice that none of things that were supposed to happen immediately have not happened in 225 years. The book says if anybody changes it he will be condemned. The attendees of the conference were scared. So they incorporated the book in the bible.

The preachers loved it. Because they could scare the people about the imminent end of the world and rapture and millennium of Jesus's rule etc. and collect offerings and tithes. So, 2000 years later here we are trying to make sense out of psychedelic fantasy.]

OTHER BOOKS BY SAME AUTHOR

Holy Bible: Genesis (Study Bible)
Holy Bible: Exodus, (Study Bible)
Holy Bible: Leviticus, (Study Bible)
Holy Bible: Numbers, (Study Bible)
Holy Bible: Deuteronomy (Study Bible)
Gospel Of Mathew – (Study Bible)
Gospel Of Mark – (Study Bible)
Gospel Of Luke – (Study Bible)
Gospel Of John – (Study Bible)
The Revelation (Study Bible)
Holy Cow! What Did Mark write?
Was Jesus Black?
Jesus : The Eastern Star
Conversion of Terrorist
Origin of Everything - The Creationist Version
My Journey from Islam to Christianity
Pedophile Priest
Search for Mr. Almighty
A Returning Veteran
Big Black Little Blonde
Song of the Blind Girl
Lucy's Law
Trial Of A Monster
The President Goes to Heaven
Secret Codes
Who Killed Aliyah ?
Fukushima Report
Figure Skater

ABOUT THE AUTHOR

The Author has spent several years researching the Ancient Scriptures, Ancient History and Times and Practices of Ancient Civilizations and visiting locations and talking to experts and locals and those in the know.
You may contact author by e-mail at:
cindynet.marktom@yandex.ru

.

.

.

ACKNOWLEDGMENTS

The Author is obligated to many people for their contributions to the making of this book. It is difficult to thank them all by name.
Special thanks to the researchers and analysts and linguists and ancient manuscript keepers,
'*The Bodleian Libraries of the University of Oxford*',
'The Biblioteca Apostolica Vaticana (BAV)',
'*The Library of Congress*',
'The Lenin State Library of Moscow',
'*The Admont Benedictine Monastery in Austria*',
'The British Library'

.
.
.
.
.
.
.
.
.
.
.
.
.
.
.
.
.
.
.
.

Made in the USA
Monee, IL
07 January 2025